"*We* have a child. A son."

Their eyes tangled. *A son.* There was no way that Leandro was going to cave in and believe Abby but...fatherhood. It was something he had never considered. Never wanted! He'd seen from his own unstable childhood that the production of children was something that could go horribly wrong. He'd not only learned from his own experience but he'd learned from his sister's. He'd never wished to reproduce and take a chance on being a father. It wasn't in his makeup.

What if she was telling the truth? Faced with that possibility, Leandro suddenly knew what it felt like for one's world to fall apart. He'd sought order all his life, to combat the lack of order that had marked his formative years, and there could be nothing more disastrous and explosive when it came to destroying all that hard-fought-for order than the arrival of a child.

But, no, he wasn't going to think like that.

He was a cool, rational man. He forced his thoughts away from *possibilities*. *Possibilities* counted for nothing.

"Where?"

"I beg your p

"You tell me me son."

D1413691

Cathy Williams can remember reading Harlequin books as a teenager, and now that she is writing them, she remains an avid fan. For her, there is nothing like creating romantic stories and engaging plots, and each and every book is a new adventure. Cathy lives in London, and her three daughters—Charlotte, Olivia and Emma—have always been, and continue to be, the greatest inspirations in her life.

Books by Cathy Williams

Harlequin Presents

Bought to Wear the Billionaire's Ring
Snowbound with His Innocent Temptation
A Virgin for Vasquez
Seduced into Her Boss's Service
The Wedding Night Debt
A Pawn in the Playboy's Game
At Her Boss's Pleasure
The Real Romero
The Uncompromising Italian
The Argentinian's Demand
Secrets of a Ruthless Tycoon
Enthralled by Moretti
His Temporary Mistress

The Italian Titans

Wearing the De Angelis Ring
The Surprise De Angelis Baby

One Night With Consequences

Bound by the Billionaire's Baby

Seven Sexy Sins

To Sin with the Tycoon

Visit the Author Profile page at Harlequin.com for more titles.

Cathy Williams

THE SECRET
SANCHEZ HEIR

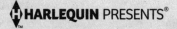

ISBN-13: 978-0-373-06071-9

The Secret Sanchez Heir

First North American Publication 2017

Copyright © 2017 by Cathy Williams

Printed in U.S.A.

THE SECRET
SANCHEZ HEIR

CHAPTER ONE

THROUGH THE WINDOWS of the airy den tucked away in the west wing of his sprawling country mansion, Leandro Sanchez had a bird's eye view of what could only be called the inevitable end of his six-month relationship with Rosalind Duval.

Only fitting, he thought, that a high-maintenance, spoiled diva should exit on a cloud of over-the-top drama.

It was a little after six in the evening and the last of the trucks that only that morning had delivered food, decorations—including a ridiculous ice sculpture for display in his hall—and several dozen staff was now departing. The specially bought Chinese-style lanterns that lined the long, private avenue leading up to his estate twinkled and glittered in the lightly falling snow and illuminated the dark shapes of the vehicles slowly wending their way away from his estate.

Sensual mouth compressed into a thin line of distaste, Leandro replayed in his mind the events of the last three hours. He had returned from his business trip to New York, fresh off the red eye, to pick up a barrage of text messages from Rosalind that he was to come immediately to his country house where he would find a surprise waiting for him.

Leandro loathed surprises. He was especially put out because, during the past week while he had been in New York, he had decided that his relationship with the very eligible Lady Rosalind Duval had reached the end of its course.

On paper, she had ticked all the boxes. She was beautiful, well-bred and independently wealthy. Her parents, whilst not nearly on the same level as him financially, formed the bedrock of that dying breed known as the British aristocracy. As a bonus, she was friendly with his sister Cecilia, who, indeed, had engineered the initial meeting between them.

Leandro was not in the market for love but he had been…*restless* and Rosalind had stepped into that uncustomary void with the promise of something *different*. It was not to be.

Her background had filled her with high expectations that every single one of her demands would be met with complete subservience. As a privileged only child, she was accustomed to getting her own way, and the fact that she was in her early thirties proved no barrier to her stamping her feet and throwing temper tantrums if things didn't go as she decreed. She had always been the centre of attention and had seen no reason why he, Leandro, shouldn't fall in line and continue the tradition.

She'd demanded his constant attention, phoning him sometimes several times a day and, having had full use of his credit card, had seen absolutely nothing wrong with buying whatever she'd happened to fancy on a whim. From jewellery, to clothes, to an outrageously expensive sports car, finally to an *engagement ring* which, he had discovered to his horror, had been the surprise waiting for him when he had returned from New York.

'Special delivery!' She had beamed as hordes of people came and went, fetching, carrying and getting everything in place for the accompanying engagement party which had been arranged for the following day. 'It should arrive at just the right time for us to pop a cork and celebrate before dinner. It's time we made this official, Leandro. Mummy and Daddy are simply *desperate* for a grandchild and I don't see the point of delaying any longer. We're both in our thirties and it's time to take the next step. Darling, I *know* you're a typical man and wouldn't dream of doing anything about it, so I thought I'd do the necessary!'

He watched the tail end of the last van disappear from view then, flexing his lean muscles, he strolled out towards the kitchen, taking in the detritus left behind in the wake of everyone's hasty departure.

In the hall, the ridiculous ice sculpture of a couple entwined was still perfectly intact and would require removal the following day. He would have to enlist a team of cleaners to return his country house to its 'before' state.

Right now, all he wanted was something strong to drink. The wretched engagement ring was on its way. Another hasty departure would have to be effected, although he was debating whether he would keep the ring or not. It had cost a small fortune. Quite a flawless diamond, he had seen from the receipt that had been flung at him by an incandescent Rosalind. Maybe he would gift it to her. She had, after all, been responsible for sourcing the priceless gem even if it *had* been purchased on *his* credit card.

He grimaced and thought that there was a better than even chance that the gesture would not be met with warm approval.

For once, his thoughts assumed an introspective nature. In the kitchen, Julie, his housekeeper, was busy trying to eradicate all evidence of the blighted party preparations. He dismissed her while he poured himself a drink.

'One more delivery due,' he said absently, swirling the amber liquid in the glass and staring down at it for a few seconds before glancing across to the middle-aged woman who had been responsible for looking after his country mansion for the past five years, ever since he had bought it. 'I will need to dispatch this one personally. I'll be in my office. When the courier arrives, let me know, Julie. They shouldn't be on the premises for longer than ten minutes and then you can leave for the evening. You'll need the usual team here in the morning to finish clearing up this…mess.'

It annoyed him that he was still unable to rein in his wandering mind, because he was a man who had little or no time for pointless raking over the past. Yet now, as he strolled back towards his office, closing his curtains against a view of snow that was falling thicker and faster, he couldn't stop himself from thinking.

Thinking about Rosalind and the chain of events that had brought her into his life and contrived to keep her there, even though, almost from the very start, he had seen the cracks begin to appear.

His sister, Cecilia, had been instrumental in bringing about their meeting and he knew, in a vague way, she'd been instrumental in making him hesitate before doing what had to be done. He sighed, already predicting what his sister's reaction would be when she received the inevitable phone call from

Rosalind, who would surely speak to Cecilia before he had had time to fill her in himself.

He swallowed back the remainder of the whisky in his glass, sat down, pushing the chair away from the big, old-fashioned mahogany desk, and thought back…back to events of eighteen months previously and to another woman who had swept into his life for a matter of weeks and wreaked havoc.

Gold-digger…liar…*thief*…

He had had a narrow escape, had walked away from her without looking back, and it infuriated him to know that, however far and fast he walked, she was still there like a thorn in his side, making itself felt at the slightest opportunity. He hadn't been able to escape her and, in ways he couldn't put his finger on but knew existed, she had been responsible for that lethal restlessness that had made him question the direction his life had been taking. Questions which had subsequently lowered his defences when it had come to contemplating something of a more permanent nature with a woman who'd actually appeared to fit the bill.

His jaw clenched and he swung back to his computer, blanking out his memories of the golden-haired, green-eyed witch who had made him take his eye off the ball. There was no point in resurrecting the past. It was over and done with. Once he had sent the courier delivering the ring on his way back down to London, his chapter with Rosalind would be at an end and life, as always, would carry on.

On that note, he did what he did best—buried himself in work—and, within ten minutes, thoughts of the past were where they should be: locked away and incapable of jumping out at him, at least for the moment.

Abigail Christie was running late. The driver, a trusted employee of Vanessa—Abigail's boss, who had saved her, in a manner of speaking, and who owned the exquisite, upmarket jeweller's from which Lady Rosalind Duval had purchased the diamond—had been under strict instructions to *make it to Greyling Manor no later than five, under penalty of death*. Unfortunately, those instructions had allowed no leeway for the twin assault of vile weather and the accompanying stop-start traffic. They had left an overcast London bang on time but had run into problems the second they had hit Oxford and, from there on, it had been a frustrating race against the clock.

Abigail had not been able to contact Lady Rosalind to advise her of the delay because she hadn't been picking up.

The only silver lining was the fact that, although they were now over two hours behind schedule, they had finally left most of the traffic behind and, whilst the country lanes leading to Greyling Manor might be dark, twisty and frankly treacherous given the weather conditions, their destination was at last within touching distance.

She would thrust the ring at Lady Rosalind, get her signature as fast as she could and leave without further ado.

Doubtless, Rosalind Duval would be waiting with bated breath for them to arrive and would be as keen to see the back of them as they would be to see the back of Greyling Manor, which was buried deep in the heart of the Cotswolds.

No sticking around to gather themselves before embarking on the return journey. No polite conversation with the lord of the manor and no having to contend with whatever arrogant, Hooray Henry types had gathered in preparation for tomorrow's Big Reveal and would want to have a preview of the magnificent engagement ring. Not now that they were running so late. And that afforded Abigail a great deal of relief because the prospect of dipping her toes back into the waters of that rarefied world of the super-rich was something that made her feel physically sick.

It had revived all the worst memories she had of just how unscrupulous the people who inhabited that world could be. She had had her disastrous brush with how the other half lived and she was in no hurry for a return visit.

Indeed, she had done her best to get out of delivering this ring, not least because she hadn't handled the sale. She had only seen Rosalind in passing, but the timing had been bad for Vanessa and typical of a young, rich woman who snapped her fingers and expected all her wishes to be met instantly, Rosalind had set a date for the delivery and had refused to budge.

And there were other reasons why Abigail intended to tell Hal, the driver, to keep the engine running while she flew in, did what was necessary and flew back out.

For the fourth time in under an hour, she checked her phone for any communication from her friend Claire, but a reliable network service had died pretty much as soon as they had hit the first winding country lane and it hadn't got any better the deeper into the heart of the Cotswolds they had travelled.

With a sigh of frustration, Abigail leant back and watched the dark scenery drift past her. There was something eerie about the veil of snow falling steadily into the inky-black landscape, settling over the open fields. She was accustomed to light pollution and the constant sounds of a city. Out here, she felt as though she could have been on another planet, and she didn't like that because it made her think of

Sam, her ten-month-old son back in London, and the fact that he would be fast asleep by the time she made it back to her house, even if the turnaround here was faster than the speed of light.

And then, hard on the heels of that, she started to think about the weather, started to wonder whether she was imagining it or whether the snow was getting thicker. It was so hard to tell in the darkness. What if these little lanes became impassable? Right now, they seemed fine, but what if she couldn't make it back to London? She would have to find a bed and breakfast somewhere, and that would entail an overnight stay, and she had never spent a night away from Sam. She couldn't imagine not waking up in the morning to the sound of his gurgling and little complaining cries that went on until she scooped him up for his morning bottle.

Lost in thought, she surfaced when the vehicle slowed, turned through impressive wrought-iron gates and headed up a long, tree-lined drive that was lit by a series of lanterns. It was beautifully romantic and it was only as they approached the Georgian mansion that she felt the first stirrings of unease.

The place looked deserted, aside from a couple of cars in the circular courtyard. Most of the house was in darkness and she made Hal double check to make sure he had got the address right.

'You'd better come in with me,' she said dubiously

and Hal, killing the engine, turned round and looked at her, his cheerful face serious.

'If this is an engagement party,' he said in his usual direct fashion, 'then I'll eat my hat.' He waved the woollen hat lying on the seat next to him and grinned. 'I've seen more life in a graveyard.'

'Don't say that. I have a ring to deliver. Vanessa will be distraught if for some reason the sale falls through.'

'It won't, love.' He smiled kindly at her. 'You'll probably find that the action will kick off tomorrow. That's when the party's due to take place, isn't it? The happy couple are probably just relaxing and enjoying some peace before the big day ahead.'

Ten minutes later, Abigail discovered that that couldn't have been further from the truth.

Leandro had thoroughly cleared his head of the catastrophic mess that had awaited him when he had arrived back from New York. That was the joy of work. It put everything into perspective. It was a world in which everything was clear cut and everything had a solution. Now, as Julie popped her head round the door to inform him that the last link in the 'belly up' chain had arrived, bearing the ill-fated ring, Leandro was obliged to face the final annoying hurdle in putting this matter to rest.

He was, fortunately, in a better frame of mind.

Rosalind had shouted and screamed, furious that for the first time in her life someone had scuppered her plans. She had threatened social exclusion, at which point Leandro had made the mistake of laughing, and she had been apoplectic when he had suggested that she was far better off without him, because he simply didn't have the reserves of energy or patience to give her the sort of attention she required. Nor, he had added, had he the slightest interest in having children. In fact, he could think of nothing worse. So the pitter-patter of tiny feet would have remained an unfulfilled ambition.

Rosalind had got the worst out of her system and he felt that, when she eventually descended from her rage, she would find blessed relief in gossiping about him behind his back and painting whatever picture it took for her to emerge smelling of roses.

For his part, burying himself in work had put everything in perspective.

He had no idea what had driven him to imagine that anything could be more important. His abiding memory of his parents was of two spoiled and wealthy people caught up in a hedonistic whirl, incapable of growing up and certainly incapable of looking after the child they had accidentally conceived. Even less had they been able to deal with the arrival of Cecilia years later, another accident. The task of taking care of his much younger sister had fallen to him and, from a young age, Leandro had worked out that the tumult of emotion and the chaos it was capable of engendering was not for him. A healthy aversion to chaos, disorder and unpredictability had been ingrained in him from a tender age.

As a teenager, he had lost himself in his studies, only surfacing to make sure his sister was okay. As an adult, work had replaced the studies, and when his parents had died, victims of their wild, irresponsible lifestyle—speedboat racing at night in the Caribbean—work had become even more imperative because he had had to rescue what was left of the family finances. There had been no time to kick back and relax. Work was and always would be the most important driving force of Leandro's life. Rosalind's hysterics had clarified that for him.

He had told Julie to show the courier into the smallest of the sitting rooms, the one which bore the least evidence of the party that wasn't going to be taking place. He now made his way there, mind half on the business proposal he had been reading before he had been interrupted.

On tenterhooks, because whatever was wrong was *very, very* wrong and the fast exit she had been hoping for now seemed out of the question, Abigail was sitting upright in a chair in the room into which she had been delivered like an unwanted parcel.

Rosalind was, she was given to understand, not there. Hal was to wait in the kitchen where he would be given something to eat and she was to wait for the master of the house in the sitting room where, she hoped, he would take delivery of the ring.

She heard the approach of footsteps on the marble floor and was already rising to her feet, having rehearsed what she needed to say about getting back to London urgently before the weather took a turn for the worse.

Whatever the heck was going on, it wasn't her problem. She had already reached that conclusion. She'd done her job and, if the loved-up couple had had a tiff, then that was nothing to do with her.

She didn't know who or what to expect. Stiff with tension, with the metal box containing the ring clutched to her chest, for a few seconds Abigail almost thought that her nerves had brought on a hallucinatory attack.

Because there was no way that those footsteps she had heard could possibly have heralded the arrival of a six-foot-two specimen of pure, hard-edged masculinity. There was no way that those achingly familiar tawny eyes, fringed by eyelashes she had once teased could have been the envy of any woman, could now be staring at her. *It just wasn't possible.* Leandro Sanchez *could not* be lounging in the doorway of this sitting room, larger than life.

She couldn't tear her eyes away from him. He was her very worst nightmare and her very deepest, darkest, most forbidden fantasy come to life and she blinked, desperately hoping that the vision would disappear. It didn't. He remained just where he was, an alpha male of such sinful beauty that he took her breath away. He had taken her breath away the first time she had seen him a year and a half ago. Over the weeks of their torrid and doomed love affair, that impact had never lessened.

He was the sort of guy women dreamed about. Olive-skinned, tawny-eyed and with an electrifying, ruthless sex appeal. He was long, lean and muscular, and Abigail thought that she could remember each and every muscle and sinew of that fabulous body.

She had never thought that she'd see him again, not after *everything,* and as the full horror of this accidental encounter hit home the room began to swim. She felt nausea rise in a tide up her throat, and she swallowed back the bile, but she couldn't seem to stop herself from swaying. She felt her legs give way and knew that she was going to pass out before she hit the ground.

She came to on one of the low, cream sofas facing the arched window through which she had been absently gazing only seconds before and struggled up to find that Leandro had dragged a chair over by the sofa and was sitting, watching her.

'Drink this.' He pressed a glass with some brandy into her hand and forced her to take a sip. His eyes were cool and guarded, his hand was steady, his voice controlled.

Not a single thing conveyed his utter shock at walking into the room and coming face to face with the only woman who had got under his skin and refused to budge—and, as if that wasn't sufficiently appalling, it galled him to realise that his ability to recall had been spot-on because she was just as exquisite as he remembered.

Her hair was just as colourful and, from what he could tell, just as long, although right now it was pinned back severely in a bun. Her eyes were as green as he remembered, green with gold flecks that were only apparent when you really took time to look, which he had. Her figure was as luscious and as sexy, a figure that could haunt a man's dreams.

Of their own accord, his eyes drifted down, lingering on the full swell of her breasts pushing against the drab white blouse, and the length of her legs primly hidden under a pair of grey trousers. She was dressed in high street fashion. Wherever life had taken her since they had parted company, it certainly hadn't been into the open arms of another billionaire.

'Leandro…this can't be happening…' She would have stood up except her legs had turned to jelly.

'You're in my house, you're sitting on my sofa.' He stood up and strolled towards the fireplace, putting some distance between them, every nerve in his body electrified by the shock of finding her in his house. 'It's happening all right. I take it that you're the courier with the ring?'

'I… Yes… I am.' Abigail's eyes skittered towards him and just as quickly skittered away. She reached for the metal safety-deposit box and held it out to him. Leandro ignored the gesture.

Propelled into nervous speech, Abigail gave him a stilted, jerky explanation for being in his house, all the while feeling like an unwary rabbit that had suddenly strayed into the path of a voracious predator.

'It seems…' Leandro sauntered back towards her, eyes narrowed as he watched her cringe back against the sofa. As she should, he thought, considering the last time they had been in one another's company she had been revealed for the liar and thief that she was. '…that your boss got the wrong end of the stick.'

'I beg your pardon?'

'That ring was purchased without my consent. Unfortunately, Rosalind misinterpreted the depth of our relationship.'

'But we were told that there was to be an engagement party…'

Leandro shrugged and continued looking at her as he sat back down on the chair that he had pulled over, which was far too close for comfort, as far as Abigail was concerned. 'Crossed wires all round,' he informed her coolly.

'So is Rosalind...? Has Rosalind...?' Abigail struggled to make sense of the situation while her thoughts kept whirling round in utter confusion and her body burned and tingled as though she'd been plugged in to a live socket.

'I never had plans to marry her.' Leandro brushed aside the question with just a hint of impatience. Now that she was sitting here in his living room, larger than life and just as sexy, all those memories he had carefully locked away were coming out to play. He remembered the way she had felt, the noises she'd made when he'd touched her, the way their bodies had fit together like one. He'd bumped into ex-girl-friends before and had felt nothing for them but a sense of relief that they were no longer around. He certainly had never looked at them and *wanted* them.

But then no other relationship had ended the way theirs had...

Jittery and feeling caged in, Abigail sprang to her feet and began pacing the room nervously, hands clasped behind her back, barely able to think straight. 'So this trip has been a complete waste of time. What am I supposed to do now? With the ring?' *Focus on why you're here,* she told herself feverishly, *and forget about everything else.*

'Now that you've made the effort to bring it here, you'd better let me have a look—see where my hard-earned money has gone.' He nodded to the box and Abigail dutifully extracted the ring with shaking fingers and watched as he carefully held it up to the light and inspected it.

'It's not my problem if you've broken off your engagement with Lady Rosalind,' she said jerkily.

'I haven't *broken* anything off. There was never an engagement to break off. She bought this off her own bat because she wanted to pin me down. The strategy didn't work. I'd already decided to finish with her before I knew anything about this ridiculous scheme and that's exactly what I did when I returned here after my trip abroad.'

Abigail shivered because this was just the sort of ruthless side to him she had finally glimpsed when their relationship had crashed and burned.

She thought of Sam and was overcome with sudden sickening fear and apprehension. 'The ring was sold in good faith,' she told him flatly, taking a deep breath and exhaling slowly because it steadied her shattered nerves. 'I just need you to sign for the delivery and then I can be out of here.'

'Really?' Leandro relaxed, crossing his legs and leaning back in his chair. 'Why the rush?'

'Why do you think, Leandro?' Abigail asked in a high-pitched voice. 'The last time we met you were walking out of your apartment, leaving me with your sister, believing every word she had said about me being a liar, a thief and a gold-digger. So, believe it or not, the less time I spend in your company, the better. If I'd known that you were the man Lady Rosalind was about to marry, there's no way I would have come all the way here to deliver a ring. But I didn't, and now the ring is in your possession, and all I need is your signature before I leave.'

'I'm not going to go down the road of reminiscing over your lies and half-truths,' Leandro told her calmly. 'As for the ring... I may or may not decide to keep it.'

'You have to!' Abigail gasped. 'Vanessa has just taken over her father's business and this sale is a real coup for her. There was stiff competition from other buyers to get hold of this particular diamond!'

'Not my problem, although it beggars belief that you managed to con your way into a job handling priceless jewellery, now that we're on the subject. Does your employer know that you're prone to being light-fingered?'

'I don't have to stay and listen to this!'

'Oh, but you do. Or have you forgotten that you need my signature?' He snapped shut the box with a definitive click. 'I think I'll keep it,' he decided briskly, 'as an investment. It'll make me money. Now, sit.'

'I have to go.'

Leandro looked at her narrowly as she glanced down at her watch with just the slightest hint of panic, as she licked her lips and fidgeted.

'It took much longer to get here than I anticipated,' Abigail said into the growing silence. 'We should have arrived ages ago, at least two hours ago, but the weather... I'd planned on being back in London by eight-thirty. I really have to get back...'

'Why?' he asked smoothly. 'Glass slipper going to get lost? Carriage about to turn into a pumpkin? There's no wedding ring on your finger, so I take it that there's no Mr Right keeping the fires burning on the home front. Or is there?' He found that he didn't care for the thought of a man in Abigail's life and that streak of inappropriate possessiveness shocked him.

But then, why beat about the bush? She'd lodged in his head like a burr and the plain truth was that he still wanted her. It made no sense, because she represented everything he found distasteful, but for reasons he couldn't begin to understand she still turned him on. Something about the way she was put together. He'd been out with some of the most beautiful women in the world and none of them could get to him the way this one could.

It was as infuriating as it was undeniable.

She was still in his system, a slither of unfinished business, and there was only one way he could think of to get her out of his system once and for all.

He lowered his eyes and felt the kick of satisfaction at a decision taken. It would be an insult to fate, which had decided to throw them together, were he not to take advantage of the situation.

'It's none of your business whether there's someone in my life or not, Leandro!' Agitated, she sprang to her feet, challenging him to stop her. 'Now, if you'll excuse me, Hal is waiting in the kitchen. I'll go fetch him and we can head off. It took us hours to get here, and it'll probably take us hours to get back, and I...'

'And you...what?'

'Nothing,' she muttered. 'I just need to go now.'

'By all means, although...' he nodded towards the window '...you might want to reconsider that decision. If you look outside, you'll find that the weather conditions that delayed your trip here are now considerably worse. Leave here and you're liable to end up in a ditch by the side of the road somewhere. That's the thing with these country lanes—they're very picturesque in summer but positively lethal in winter when the weather decides to take a turn for the worse.'

Abigail paled and followed the direction of his gaze, then she anxiously went to the window and peered outside. The flakes were raining down fast and thick. Already, the extensive grounds of the country estate were carpeted in white. It was beautiful. It was also, she noted with sickening dismay, virtually impassable.

'I can't stay here. I have to get back!'

'Feel free. But perhaps that should be a joint decision taken with your driver.'

'You don't understand! *I have to get back to London tonight.*'

'You're not going anywhere,' Leandro told her. 'This snow is going to get worse before it gets better. You might be willing to put your life at risk in your desperate need to return to the city, but you have your driver to consider. Frankly, what you choose to do with your life is entirely your concern, but I won't be responsible for any accident that might befall your driver. I will ensure that he is fed and settled into one of the guest suites for the night. By tomorrow, you will doubtless find that the driving conditions are improved.'

Abigail was close to tears but there was nothing she could do. 'I can't get a signal on my phone,' she told him, defeated. 'I need to make a call.'

Leandro didn't say anything but he was thinking fast. A man? Not a husband, but a lover? Who else? And would that stop him? He wanted her, but was that want reciprocated?

He had one night, he thought with satisfaction, and one night should be more than enough to put this urge to bed once and for all. He would find out soon enough.

CHAPTER TWO

ABIGAIL HAD EXPECTED similar alarm from Hal about being trapped at Greyling Manor for the night—he was a family man with three young children—but he seemed pleased as punch not to be returning to London.

'Treacherous roads,' he said comfortably as he settled in front of the array of wildly extravagant food which had been laid on for them by Leandro's housekeeper. 'Wouldn't want to risk driving on them, and besides, I haven't been out of London in months.'

While he had tucked into the surplus party grub, with Julie nodding approvingly at his hearty appetite, Abigail toyed worriedly with her food. She had, at least, managed to get through to her friend Claire who was looking after Sam for the evening, and she had cheerfully agreed to stay until she returned.

'I'll be back no later than tomorrow lunchtime,' Abigail had said *sotto voce*, for she had been directed to the landline and was petrified that Leandro might be lurking behind a door and overhearing her conversation. 'I don't care *what* the weather decides to do. There's no way I can stay here.'

'I know you miss Sam,' her friend had said soothingly, 'but it's better for you to wait and travel back when it's safe rather than risk life and limb. I promise to take very good care of the little guy!'

Abigail knew that her friend would. She had met Claire at the handful of antenatal classes they had attended together, and they had hit it off immediately. Both young, both single and both pregnant. Although, in Claire's case, she had had a job at the local nursery. Thanks to Claire, Abigail had managed to get Sam registered and, much as she had hated leaving him there when he had only been four months old, she'd had to in order to work to keep the roof over both their heads. Knowing that Claire was there, looking after him every bit as thoroughly as she looked after her own son, had helped a lot. Just as Vanessa had given her a job when she had needed it most, so too had Claire chipped in and helped her with Sam when she'd needed it.

Claire had no idea where Abigail was and neither did she know why she so desperately needed to leave.

So far, she had inspected the weather a dozen times in the space of the past two hours.

There was some let up but not much. She had

barely been able to touch a morsel of food and was only thankful that Leandro had disappeared into the bowels of the house. There was a slim chance that she wouldn't see him again but she knew that that would make little difference to the onslaught of memories, heartache and misgivings that had risen to the surface, like debris washed ashore.

Of course you could never forget the past, but now the scab that had been formed had been picked apart to expose the barely healed wound underneath.

As Hal was shepherded up to his quarters, as happy as a privileged guest in a five-star hotel, Abigail remained in the kitchen with her cup of coffee, remembering the past she had tried to put behind her.

She could recall the very second she had looked up and seen Leandro standing in front of her, so unbelievably gorgeous that her mouth had run dry and every single thought had fled her head. In that split second, she had forgotten all about the job she had just failed to secure, the uncertain future staring her in the face, the last laugh her philandering, lecherous ex-boss had had at her expense by insinuating in his reference that she had been sacked for theft. She had turned down the pass he had made, had allowed her disgust to show and had paid the price.

She had been at rock bottom. Every single effort she had ever made to elevate herself and get away from a background that had been a slideshow of foster homes and indifferent adults had been for nothing.

Then she had felt a shadow, looked up and there he'd been, all big, brooding and heart-stoppingly gorgeous, and for the first time in her life Abigail had discovered the meaning of sexual chemistry.

She'd spent so many years playing down her looks, telling herself that she would never, *ever* allow anyone into her life because they wanted to have sex with her, and fending off unwanted advances from the age of thirteen, that she'd been quite unprepared to discover that sexual attraction had no time at all for pep talks and earnest lectures.

Indeed, sexual attraction hadn't given a damn about her resolve never to leap into bed with a man who wanted her for her body and not much else. Her mother had been that woman before an overdose had ended her life. Abigail had known that she would never end up selling herself short like her mother had. Unfortunately, the power of that same sexual attraction she had had under tight control had refused to obey her ground rules. It had raced out of the box in which it had been contained with the gusto of a racehorse sprinting from the starting box.

Leandro hadn't even beaten around the bush. He'd just said, conversationally, that it was nearly lunchtime and he knew a nice little Italian just round the corner. He had not bothered to wrap up what he'd wanted in fancy packaging. She'd bowled him over, he had said over lunch, looking at her with those fabulous, long-lashed eyes, the very casualness of his voice at odds with what he was saying. He didn't do commitment, he'd made it clear, but he wanted her and he was going to New York. He'd glanced at his watch with a nonchalance she'd found unutterably *cool* and had told her he wanted to take her with him, but that she'd have to decide on the spot, because his private jet was due to leave in three hours.

His eyes had roved over her with open desire but everything about him had told her that, if she chose to walk away, he wouldn't try to stop her.

He'd been *everything* she hadn't been looking for and she'd dumped every single principle she'd ever had and gone with him. She'd let him sweep her into his world of chauffeur-driven cars, five-star hotels and every whim granted at the snap of a finger. He'd worked during the day and had insisted that she buy herself a new wardrobe, and whatever else she fancied in whatever store she chose, because money was no object.

But she *had* objected, only to learn that, what Leandro didn't want to hear, he simply chose to ignore, and he hadn't wanted to hear her objections.

'I have never,' he had told her, undressing her very, very slowly, 'allowed any woman of mine to pay for anything. Not going to change the habit now.'

No-strings-attached sex was what he'd offered and it was what she'd taken, greedy for him in a way that had shocked her beyond words. They'd lived for the moment and, whilst she had not lied to him about her past, neither had she told him about it. Somewhere along the line, she'd felt that it would turn him off and quite quickly she'd known that she hadn't wanted to turn him off.

When one week had turned into two and then three, and when, on the spur of the moment, he had decided to take a break with her in the wilds of Canada, she'd begun to hope that what had started out as just sex might end up as more.

But then everything had gone wrong, and it had all happened so fast. One minute she had been dreaming impossible dreams, and the next minute his sister had entered the frame and within three days all her fledgling dreams had lain in ruins around her and she'd been turfed out of his Manhattan apartment without a backward glance.

He'd made no bones about spelling out the sort of unscrupulous guy he was when it came to women and, instead of listening, she had chosen to ignore the writing on the wall because she had been first bowled over by him and then head over heels in love with him.

Abigail stared off now into the distance. She hadn't drawn the curtains in the kitchen and she could see that, whilst the snow wasn't getting any heavier, it was still falling, a flurry of white, shining and beautiful where the lights around the house illuminated the drift.

'So...' a familiar voice drawled from behind her.

Startled, Abigail saw Leandro's reflection in the glass of the French doors through which she had been staring. He'd changed into a pair of black jeans and a long-sleeved black jumper, the sleeves of which had been pushed up to the elbows, and he was barefoot. It might be freezing outside, but this rolling country manor was heated to perfection. Her heart jumped and her mouth went dry as she turned slowly towards him.

'I see you decided to stay rather than brave the snow in an attempt to get out of here. Wise decision.'

'I thought you'd gone to bed.' Abigail said jerkily—the first thing that came to her head.

'You mean you'd *hoped* I'd gone to bed. Why's that?' Leandro strolled towards a platter of cold meats, made himself a clumsy sandwich and poured himself a glass of red wine, offering her one as well, an offer she refused.

She gazed at him helplessly as he sat at the kitchen table. She'd remembered the way his physical presence could affect her. She'd forgotten *how much*.

'It's awkward being here,' she stammered, finally

dropping into the chair opposite him and watching as he ate, his eyes flicking towards her every so often.

Leandro didn't say anything. He thought that awkward didn't begin to cover it, but the hand of fate worked in mysterious ways, and he wasn't feeling uncomfortable with the situation at all.

Indeed, things were remarkably clear cut. Far clearer cut than they had been when they had been seeing one another a year and a half ago.

Then he had found himself, for the first time in his life, in a situation in which normal play had been suspended. The rules he had always applied to his life had taken a back seat and, even before his sister Cecilia had had her say, he had known that the relationship was entering unexplored territory. When he had first laid eyes on Abigail, he had known that he wanted her. Desire had hit him hard and fast and, never one to ignore the demands of his libido, he had done what he had always done, without beating round the bush or going down any nonsensical courtship route. He'd found her attractive and he'd wanted to bed her. A simple equation.

He hadn't reckoned on her being a virgin and he wondered whether that had marked the beginning of all those subtle changes that had pulled him in and frankly terrified him at the same time.

She'd been cagey about her past and he hadn't

pressed her for detail, instinctively wanting to hang on to whatever safe ground he could. He hadn't wanted her to start the whole confiding game, which always inevitably led to the sort of cloying situation that he found a huge turn-off. He'd sought to keep her at a distance because he could feel the compulsive drag of being pulled in and, subconsciously, that had seemed the safest way of fighting it.

He'd told himself that he wasn't curious but, even while he'd been trying to hold her at arm's length, he'd wanted to know *everything* about her, had wanted that act of possession.

Perhaps his sister had heard something in the way he had talked about Abigail down the phone. Why else would she have dug up all that dirt on her? He had known that Cecilia was possessive and he had always indulged that and understood the reason for it. He had been her anchor from the day she'd been born, but even so he had seen red when she had descended on his Manhattan apartment, clutching evidence of Abigail's past, challenging him to continue seeing a woman who, if not an outright liar, had concealed the truth—and why else unless she was a gold-digger, playing the long game? He had walked away from the relationship without a backward glance. Problem was that his body hadn't quite managed to forget her.

Which was why the woman had stayed in his

head. Which was why, looking at her now, he could feel the slow burn of desire inside him.

She was unfinished business and he still wanted her. The blondes and eventually Rosalind had been sticking plaster over an open cut and now the sticking plaster had been ripped off. There was only one way the cut was going to be healed and that was to sleep for one last time with the woman who had delivered the damage.

Things were different now. He knew Abigail for who she was. Once upon a time, he had almost believed her to be the person she'd been pretending to be, but that was then. Now, he was in no danger of being sucked into anything.

'It's only awkward,' Leandro drawled, 'if you insist on dragging the past in. Personally, I'm the sort of guy who is happy to let bygones be bygones.' He shrugged. 'I'm not interested in talking about why you did what you did.'

'I didn't *do* anything,' Abigail muttered in a driven undertone. 'Okay, so I didn't tell you about my background because I didn't want to put you off. Why is that so hard for you to understand? I'm human. You were everything I wasn't and I couldn't believe that you'd even looked in my direction. I didn't want to spoil the moment and then…things started getting serious and I just never seemed to know when to sit you down and explain that you might have got the wrong idea of who I was…'

Leandro flushed darkly. 'Things *got serious* for *you*,' he corrected coolly.

Abigail nodded. 'I won't sit here and pretend that they didn't,' she told him. 'I felt things for you and, the more I felt for you, the harder it seemed to start telling you about myself and my foster homes and what it was like growing up in them.'

Her voice had sunk to a whisper and Leandro grimly fought off any inclination to feel sympathy for her. She deserved none, and too right he would have seen things slightly differently had he known just how desperate for money she had been. The only thing she hadn't lied about had been her lack of sexual experience, and he'd wondered afterwards whether she'd been saving herself for the right billionaire to come along and elevate her to the status she felt she deserved. She'd certainly taken to the high life like a duck to water.

'And what a stroke of bad luck,' Leandro murmured smoothly, 'to have ended up trying to get a job in one of the hotels I owned. The second Cecilia knew where we'd met, it would have been easy for her to work her way backwards and to have discovered the job you failed to secure because of the reference given by your ex-boss.'

'He lied.' Abigail had been so desperate to make

him understand all those long months ago when his sister had confronted him in his apartment, but now she just felt tired of finding herself repeating the same old stuff all over again. It wasn't as though he was going to listen now any more than he had then. In fact, if anything, she repulsed him more now than she would have then because, back then, they at least had been lovers and that would have counted for *something,* surely?

'Of course,' Leandro said soothingly. 'Although I wouldn't get too moral, if I were you, considering you weren't far behind in the lying stakes…'

Abigail looked away.

'And then there was a certain incident I unearthed about a spate of shoplifting for which you received a warning in the heady days of your misspent youth…'

Abigail's eyes flew to his and she blanched, because this was news to her. 'What? You had me checked out *after* we broke up?'

'Call it curiosity.' Because a part of him had wanted to believe her. He couldn't credit himself for being the fool he'd been, but then he'd never felt for any other woman what he'd ended up feeling for her. The memory of that vulnerability made his teeth clench together in frustration and anger.

'I remember that incident,' Abigail said softly. Her eyes clouded over. 'I was only twelve at the time and I was so desperate to fit in. I'd just been transferred to another foster home and...' she sighed '... I just knew that the girls there weren't going to accept me.'

Because of how she looked. It had *always* been about how she looked. Her face had attracted too much attention and, in her circumstances, attracting too much attention had never been a good thing.

'A group of us had gone into the shopping centre for the morning. I'd tagged along, happy as anything that I'd been invited to be part of the crowd. When we got there, I only realised that the reason I'd been asked along had been so that they could make fun of me. They dared me to steal some cheap costume jewellery from one of the shops. They didn't think I would, which was probably why I did.'

She glanced up at him ruefully. 'I made a hopeless shoplifter. I couldn't have been more obvious. Of course, I was caught as soon as I walked out, and hauled down to the police station and treated like a common criminal. It wasn't even as though it made a spot of difference, because when I was returned to the home I *still* ended up standing out and being ostracised. But I learned my lesson, so that's just one reason why I would *never* have stolen anything again.'

Leandro found that he didn't like thinking of her as a kid in a police station, probably confused and scared. In fact, he found himself wishing that he could find whatever policeman had taken her in and beat the living daylights out of him, which was such a crazy reaction that he almost wanted to laugh.

It struck him, in a moment of blinding clarity, that the two of them might have come from wildly different backgrounds but that they had more in common than either of them might think.

Frowning at the sudden bout of introspection, Leandro relaxed back in the chair, topped up his wine glass and looked at her with brooding intensity. 'Like I said, there's nothing to be gained from trips down memory lane. Tell me what you've been up to since we parted company.'

Abigail stilled. She licked her lips nervously and made a big effort not to look away, because that would have been a sure sign of a guilty conscience, and she *didn't* have a guilty conscience.

'I… I managed to find the job I now have.'

She cleared her throat and looked at him as evenly as she could.

'When I got back to London I was out of work, as you know, and I'd gone to a café to try and work out what to do next. I didn't know who would employ me after that reference from my ex-boss. Who was going to believe me? Anyway, while I was having a cup of coffee Vanessa came in, and there were no free tables so she asked if she could sit at mine and, well, the rest is history, so to speak.'

She looked at him wryly and then said with some

satisfaction, 'I told her all about my past and the stupid lies that had been told about me and she believed me. She gave me a job on a trial basis and it worked out brilliantly, as it happens. I seem to have a knack for selling stuff, including high-end jewellery. None of which,' she couldn't help adding, 'I have ever been tempted to stick in my handbag and take home with me.'

'And men?' Leandro decided that it was time to push on from a topic on which he had no intention of dwelling on for too long. What was done was done.

Abigail flushed a delicate pink.

'I think it's time for me to head upstairs now. I'm tired. I want to get a good night's rest because I intend to leave first thing in the morning, and if the weather is still poor then Hal and I will just have to chance it.'

She stood up and neatened her outfit, which felt inappropriate, because she was no longer here on business. Her coat was upstairs in the bedroom suite which had been allocated to her, a sumptuous space that felt nearly as big as a football field. As were her handbag and the company laptop which she had brought with her. She had no idea what Leandro had done with the ring. Maybe he would hang onto it for his future wife.

'Have there been other men?'

Abigail's breathing hitched. He stood up and

closed the distance between them. She stuck her hands behind her back because she wanted to reach out and flatten them against his broad chest and feel the hardness of muscle and sinew underneath the black jumper. She wanted to fly back in time but that was impossible.

She thought of Sam, innocently lying in his cot back in London, and the series of decisions she had made when she had discovered that she was pregnant. Fear threatened to swamp her, fear and guilt, because, although she had been torn apart at the time, wondering whether she had made the right choice to keep the pregnancy a secret from Leandro, it had been relatively easy to live with her decision because it meant she could relegate their relationship to the past. In her head, she had kept open the option to get in touch with him at some point in the future, but she had lived for the present and so that point in the future had been nothing more than theoretical.

But the future had crashed into the present, challenging that decision she had taken and filling her with dread at just how close she was now to a conflagration that could get out of control.

She wouldn't allow that to happen. Maybe she would now rethink the choices she had made but she would do that coolly and calmly. That settled her and she relaxed a little. She thought about his question. A man in her life? She wanted to burst out laughing because, between work and motherhood, she barely had time to breathe, never mind deal with the complications of a relationship. Not that she had been tempted anyway.

'No, Leandro,' she said coolly. 'I didn't rush back to London and immediately get involved with your replacement. I've been busy trying to get my career going.'

'And no time left to jump back into the dating scene?' Leandro murmured.

'Unlike you.' Abigail couldn't resist the dig. Not only had *he* jumped right back into the dating scene but he had become so involved with a woman that she had actually been led to believe that marriage was on the cards. She turned away, angry with herself for feeling hurt and jealous.

'But it didn't work,' Leandro said softly. He reached out and circled her wrist with his hand. He stroked her skin with his thumb and Abigail wanted to moan and drag her hand away but she didn't do either. Instead, she froze.

'Want to know something?' he asked as his thumb continued to do its damage. 'I understood why when I saw you today, Abby.'

'I don't know what you're talking about,' she croaked, and he smiled crookedly at her.

'Yes, you do,' he corrected gently. 'I can feel the way you're trembling right now. You're still in my system. It doesn't make any sense, because you're the last woman I should still be interested in taking to bed, but against all odds you are. Do you think it's because what we had ended under such…bizarre circumstances?'

He sounded genuinely curious and his voice was calm, neutral and conversational. In fact, she had to sift through what he had just said and replay it in her head just to establish that she hadn't misheard it.

That he still wanted to take her to bed!

She tugged her hand and he tightened his grip on it and focused on her, his fabulous eyes lazy with intent. 'Now you're going to tell me that you have no idea what I'm talking about, aren't you? Maybe you'll express horror that I could even suggest such a thing. Am I on the right track?'

Spot on, Abigail thought. She licked her lips and tried to still her racing pulse. He was still the sexiest man she had ever laid eyes on in her life, but she was not attracted to him. *Because you couldn't possibly be attracted to a man who had insulted, offended and disbelieved you.* That just didn't make sense.

But her skin was prickling and dampness had pooled between her legs. Fascinated and mesmerised, she stared at him, sucked in by the low, honeyed seductiveness of his voice.

Leandro could feel the racing of her pulse under his thumb. Her skin was so soft and his recall of her so clear. Just touching her like this made him remember how it had felt to touch her all over, to hear the little cries and whimpers she'd made as she climbed towards an orgasm, the way she'd moved and wriggled under him. He was so turned on he had to adjust his stance to try and subdue the discomfort of his arousal.

His eyes drifted downwards to her parted lips.

Abigail knew that he was going to kiss her before his mouth covered hers and her body strained towards his, as natural an instinct as a flower leaning towards a source of light. His lips, when they touched hers, detonated a series of little thrilling explosions inside her. She wanted him. She'd never stopped wanting him. She hated him and was terrified of being here, in his company, carrying a secret she knew could be as devastating as dynamite, yet she couldn't get enough of his kiss.

With a helpless little groan, her fingers curled into his jumper and she angrily pulled him towards her even as he propelled her towards the wall without breaking physical contact.

His hands were hot and hungry on her, reaching to tug the prissy white shirt free from her trousers, then pushing underneath the shirt to cup her breasts and massage them until her nipples were pushing against the lace in a desperate bid to be caressed.

Leandro was shocked at how fabulously familiar

her body was and even more shocked at how novel he still found the experience. Familiarity, in this instance, was showing no signs of breeding contempt.

He wanted, he *needed* more than just some schoolboy groping through a bra, and he discovered that his hands were shaking as he undid the tiny pearl buttons of her blouse. Given the option, he would have ripped the thing open, so desperate was he to suckle what his hands were touching, but taking his time at least had the advantage of imposing some control on his runaway libido.

Buttons finally undone, he delicately peeled aside her blouse and lifted her bra, pushing it up so that her generous breasts were on show.

'You're so beautiful,' he said in a ragged undertone. He held her breasts in his big hands and rubbed his thumbs over her nipples, watching as they promptly stood to attention, the pink tips hardening and peaking under the caress. He looked at her. 'I want you so much it hurts,' he confessed, and Abigail shuddered because this couldn't be more wrong and yet it felt so right. 'Tell me right now that you don't want me back...'

CHAPTER THREE

'WANT YOU BACK? *Want you back?*' Abigail fought the heat suffusing her body and pushed him away but her hands were shaking as she busied herself trying to rearrange her clothing.

In response, Leandro planted both hands on either side of her, caging her in, and he looked at her without batting an eyelid. 'Shameful admission, I know,' he murmured. 'But the truth, nevertheless. I know you're not acquainted with the fine art of truth telling, but personally I find it rarely pays to ignore it. And the truth is that we're still where we were a year and a half ago—burning up for one another.'

This time Abigail *did* laugh. 'How can you call me a liar in one breath and then tell me that I'm still stupid enough to fancy you in the other?' Backed against the wall, and trapped by the sheer steel wall of his body inches away from her, she folded her arms defiantly and stared at him.

'Because lust has nothing to do with whether you like someone or not.'

'Maybe not for you!'

'Shall we put that to the test? Oh, we already did. You failed.'

Abigail could feel the little nerve jumping in her neck. She should really *hate* all this cave man, macho stuff but the truth was that Leandro did it all so well. He'd always had that intensely masculine air of cool self-assurance and a careless assumption that the world would jump when he told it to. She'd found it novel, strange and a massive turn on all at the same time and she hadn't even been able to work out why. She just had.

Now, he was exercising that self-assurance again and she could feel herself getting addled.

'Leandro, this is crazy,' she muttered. 'If it hadn't been for your ex-fiancée, I wouldn't even be here. We wouldn't have met again.'

'I wish you'd stop calling her my ex-fiancée,' Leandro said irritably. 'That was all wishful thinking on her part.'

'You were very well suited.'

'Really? I had no idea you knew her.'

'Oh, stop being so sarcastic, Leandro. You know what I mean.'

Leandro flushed darkly. In the space of only a handful of weeks, she had become the only woman

CATHY WILLIAMS 53

who had never shied away from saying exactly what she thought. She hadn't been impressed into obedience and he had liked that. 'We're moving off topic here,' he drawled. 'We were talking about this thing that's still here between us. You were busy trying to pretend that there was nothing and I was on the brink of proving to you that there is.'

'I didn't say that there was...that there was *nothing*,' Abigail denied in a harried undertone. 'But whatever there is, it's inappropriate.'

'I don't care about what happened in the past,' Leandro lied smoothly. He cared all right but, in the end, this was an even better situation in a way. Shorn of emotion, this became a sating of their physical appetites and the most natural thing in the world. It was unthinkable that she would dig her heels in and deny what was obvious and, if she did, then he had every intention of using every bit of ammunition to hand to batter down her defences.

She was probably right. If she hadn't shown up on his doorstep, their paths would never have crossed again.

But she *had* shown up and he had seen in a blinding flash that she was still in his system and would always be in his system unless he did something about it.

'But I do,' Abigail said stubbornly. 'I didn't have the greatest of backgrounds, and I was a coward for not admitting that to you from the beginning, but I didn't deserve…' She looked away, bright red, teetering between calling him out for the blind loyalty to his sister which had made him judge her without giving her a fair hearing, and just running as fast as she could away from him and the crazy feelings he had stirred up in her. 'It doesn't matter,' she muttered, staring down at her feet. Her heart was beating like a drum inside her chest and her fingers were digging into her forearms as she continued to focus on the ground while his dark gold eyes raked over her.

'Look at me, Abigail.' He stood back and tilted her chin with one finger so that their eyes met. 'I wouldn't be standing here if I didn't think that there was something *inevitable* about this accidental meeting.' Eyes still on her, he carefully traced her collarbone, and she was helpless to do anything about it. 'What happened to end things happened, and the truth is that they would have ended at some point anyway.' Something stirred uneasily inside him and he frowned briefly. 'If it's any consolation,' he confessed gruffly, 'it did make me realise how possessive my sister had become over the years without my realising.'

'Really?' Abigail's eyes widened because this was some admission, coming from a guy who would sooner have all his teeth yanked out with pliers than admit to any form of weakness, and admitting that he had allowed his sister to take control—and had misjudged the situation—was a form of weakness.

Not that it made a blind bit of difference because, as he said, things would have ended anyway. She had fallen in love with a man for whom things were always going to end. She was always going to reach a sell-by date.

'Family dynamics.' He shrugged as he realised how easy it still would be to be lulled into thinking that she was someone she wasn't. 'Will you let me see you?'

'I beg your pardon?' Now that she wasn't caged in, Abigail knew that she could terminate this conversation and briskly walk towards the door, head for her bedroom, lock herself in and make sure that she left the following day without laying eyes on him. Instead, she heard herself saying, 'I don't know what you mean.'

'Take off your shirt. I loathe that shirt anyway. Very prim and proper and we both know that you can be the opposite of prim and proper.'

'Leandro…'

'I've always loved it when you said my name like that—in that breathy, husky voice of yours.' His words were like a physical caress, pulling memories from where they had been hidden and wreaking havoc with her prized common sense.

'There's nothing wrong with my shirt.'

'There's everything wrong with it. All those infernal buttons. Very starched and white.'

'It's my work outfit.'

'I hate it and I'd really like you to take it off.'

'I can't believe you're saying that, Leandro.' But she wondered why she was surprised when he had always been the king of the outrageous demand.

His voice was as smooth as caramel and he made everything sound so easy. Two people, no strings attached, no thorny past to contend with, thrown together *for a purpose*. He almost made it sound as though it would be an insult to fate were they not to take the opportunity to jump right back into bed with one another simply because they happened to be unexpectedly sharing the same space.

Her mouth was still tingling from his hungry kiss, and her whole body was on fire, and the worst of it was that he knew it. He knew it because he *knew her*. She might have kept stuff from him—not through design but by default, almost—but really she had opened up to him in ways she'd never dreamed she would.

He had known what she thought about everything under the sun, and he'd certainly known how she'd felt when he touched her, when he'd whispered into her ear. That was why he knew exactly what was going on inside her and was certainly part of the reason why her feet seemed to be nailed to the floor and her wilful body was determined not to listen to calm reason and get the heck out of the kitchen and away from him.

'Or…'

His voice lingered seductively on that one syllable, stretching it out till her nerves were on the point of shredding.

'I could always do the taking off for you… Will you let me?'

Rendered speechless, Abigail just stared and he grinned and tilted his handsome head to one side. 'You're not saying anything. Either you've decided to consent through silence or else I take your breath away. Maybe both.'

'You are *so* full of yourself, Leandro Sanchez.'

'I know,' he said ruefully, 'and, believe me, it's something I'm trying to cure.'

'How can you flirt with me when you don't even like me?'

'I don't know,' Leandro replied with a lot more honesty than he'd intended. 'Let's stop talking.' He began to undo the buttons she had fastidiously done up only moments before and she felt her knees buckling as she let him.

His hands were very gentle on her, barely brushing her skin as he eased the shirt off and then unhooked the bra from the back and removed it. He'd moved closer to her and the only indication that he was turned on was his unsteady breathing and the hot, drowsy look in his eyes.

Abigail knew that if she touched him through his jeans she would feel the rock-hard length of his arousal, and just thinking that chipped away even more at her non-existent defences. Hard on the heels of that thought came another memory, the memory of how he filled her up, the surge of sensation as he thrust inside her, moving and building a rhythm that had never failed to take her over the top.

Pressed against the kitchen door, she arched back and her eyelids fluttered as he lowered himself down in front of her. It had been so long and, yes, she had missed this so much. It was a bitter pill to swallow because it defied all logic, but he was right. She could still want him, *want this,* even though their relationship had collapsed, even though there was no affection left between them, but instead the biggest secret of all that had the power to blow his world apart.

That secret should have stopped her but by the time his mouth was sucking on her nipple she was already too far gone into a world of heightened sensation where nothing mattered but what he was doing to her.

She plunged her hands into his hair and then half-groaned and sagged back as his questing mouth travelled lower, tracing her stomach then pausing as he reached her no-nonsense grey trousers, which doubtless he also loathed.

All those muddled thoughts were zooming around in her head as he began to unzip them, tugging them gently down until they pooled at her feet.

Her fingers were still entwined in his dark, springy hair, her eyes were shut and she could barely breathe as he pressed his face against her underwear, breathing her in.

He'd introduced her body to the art of making love and she could remember the way she had jerked back when he had first gone down there. She hadn't been able to imagine such an intimacy, but she had quickly become a fan, and her body now quivered in anticipation of his mouth and tongue delving into her. She was so turned on.

He nuzzled for a while, breathing her in, then delicately he pulled down her panties and she shimmied obligingly out of them. Her body was incredibly familiar even though Leandro dimly registered that she was slightly more rounded than he remembered. If possible, that made her even sexier. Her hips were fuller and her belly was still flat but slightly softer.

Same musky scent, though, that had always been able to work on him like a drug.

He placed his hands on her inner thighs and gently eased them apart and then he flicked his tongue

into her, finding the tight, throbbing bud and tick-
ling it until she was melting.

He wanted to pleasure her so badly it hurt. He
craved the feeling of her coming against his mouth
and he continued to lick and suck while her stifled
whimpers turned into low, barely audible groans, and
then she was coming, her spine arching, her whole
body stiffening and flailing as she couldn't hold on
any longer.

Abigail practically collapsed against him. Her climax was so explosive that it blew her legs from under
her. Hot, naked and shaking, she clung to him and
Lord knew what would have happened next in that
scenario if the shrill sound of the landline hadn't interrupted what had been, as she came to realise faster
than a bolt of lightning, a moment of complete and
utter madness.

Leandro swore under his breath and stalked across
to snatch the receiver of the kitchen phone up, at
which point he had a brusque and intensely irritated
conversation with someone who seemed to be calling from a catering company.

By the time he turned round, Abigail had managed to shove her hot, disobedient body back into its
suit of armour, even though she knew that she looked
a mess—hair all over the place, lips swollen from
where she'd been thoroughly kissed and her whole
body still flushed in the aftermath of her orgasm.

Just thinking about what she'd done made her feel sick.

'I am *not*,' Leandro grated, 'seeing this!'

Abigail flinched. 'This should never have happened!' She knew just how that sounded, and she hated herself for the picture she was painting of a woman who was happy to lead a man on and then slam the doors firmly shut in his face once she'd got what she wanted. But she wasn't going to fall into his arms again. *She couldn't.* Now that sanity had been restored, there was so much at risk here that her blood ran cold just thinking about it.

She literally burned with mortification.

'Care to explain why?'

Abigail hugged herself. 'I know what you're probably thinking.'

'You have no idea what I'm thinking!'

He was now standing directly in front of her, towering and darkly, scarily angry. However much she quailed inside, and however ashamed she was at her appalling lapse of judgement, Abigail knew that she just couldn't afford to be steamrollered by Leandro. She stood her ground with shaky legs and met his glare head-on.

'It was a mistake,' she offered with choked sincerity.

'Why?'

'Because…' She opted for part of the truth 'I can't

help being turned on by you. Maybe it's because you were my first...' She went bright red but ploughed on. 'Or maybe you're right and it's because things ended...well...maybe there's some unfinished business there. I... You touched me and I... I remembered, Leandro...'

Leandro flushed darkly, swung away and hooked his thumbs into the pockets of his jeans for a few silent seconds. He didn't care to be reminded of the power of those memories because, whilst he could acknowledge that to himself, he had no intention of sharing any such admission with Abigail. To do so would have signalled a fundamental weakness he wasn't about to expose. He disliked the notion of anything or anyone having power over him and memories fitted neatly into that category.

'But it would be wrong for us to go there,' she volunteered tentatively. Part of her thought that it was rich suddenly to come out with all of this when she had only just descended from a climax that had blown her apart. She glanced down quickly to see that the bulge was still there, pushing against his jeans, and she licked her lips and hurriedly raised her eyes to catch him looking at her. 'And I'm sorry if I gave you the wrong impression.'

Leandro didn't miss a thing. If the damned phone hadn't interrupted them, he would have taken her up to his room and he would have lost himself in her. As it stood now...

He was in line for a very long, very cold shower... and afterwards?

He wanted her and he knew why she had backed away with a sudden attack of conscience. She was dwelling on what had happened between them and allowing it to get between them.

He raked his fingers through his hair and sighed. 'Why were you afraid to tell me the truth about yourself all those months ago? You can hardly blame me for reaching the conclusions I reached and acting the way I did. Concealment always carries the stench of something underhand.'

Startled, Abigail stared at him. This was the first time he had come close to giving her a chance to explain. In the aftermath of their break-up he had been happy to walk away without giving her any opportunity to defend herself.

'I told you,' she said, clearing her throat. 'I was overawed by you. I'd never met anyone like you in my life before. Also,' she added with complete honesty, 'around you I didn't feel like myself.' She grimaced, relaxing a little, because he wasn't attacking her for stringing him on when he could have been and she would have understood. She managed to get her legs to do something constructive and shuffled to one of the kitchen chairs, promptly sinking into it with relief.

'I was somebody different—somebody *normal*—and I liked how that felt. I'd spent my life being cautious around men but you swept into my life and all of that changed in a heartbeat. It was like being on a rollercoaster ride.' He strolled towards the table to join her and she raised her huge, clear, green eyes to him. 'And once I was on that ride, there was no room to raise uncomfortable topics about my past. Besides, I didn't think it would last as long as it did.'

Long enough for her to fall head over heels in love with him.

'And when it carried on…the right time just never seemed to be there.' She stood up and smoothed down her trousers, uncertain, because he had gone from rampant lover to inscrutable spectator. 'I should head up to bed now.' A glance through the window told her that the snow was still falling but lightly. She hoped for the best. She couldn't possibly stay another day in his house.

Their eyes met and for a few seconds she thought about what she had done and the secret she had kept to herself for all the right reasons. She ran through some of those reasons in her head right now. They had parted on the worst possible terms. He had never cared about her. For him, she had only ever been a short-term fling and he had never encouraged her to think otherwise. When she'd found out that she was pregnant, she had been determined to hold onto her baby, because no one had ever held on to *her*. By then, Leandro had been out of the picture.

She had imagined contacting him to give him the glad tidings, then she had gone further and wondered whether he might feel inclined to take the baby from her because, at the end of the day, he would be its father. If he'd chosen to do that, she wouldn't have stood a chance and, after the way they had broken up, he might very well have seen it as an opportunity to get some revenge for, as far as he was concerned, having been lied to.

Abigail had known that she would never risk losing her baby and, after several weeks with Leandro, she had seen for herself that he led the sort of high-octane, high-pressured lifestyle that was not compatible with living with a young child.

Fear created by dark thoughts about worst-case scenarios, heartbreak at being dumped by the guy she had fallen in love with because she wasn't good enough and hormones coursing through her system had propelled her into a decision she now realised had been a life-changing one.

Yet it had been a curiously easy decision to make in the aftermath of their relationship.

She had even told herself that it was responsible not to foist an unwanted child on a guy who had not planned for a pregnancy. Why should an inveterate bachelor be made to pay such a high price for a simple mistake?

But now, things didn't seem quite so clear cut. She expected him to try and stop her but Leandro remained where he was, watching as she headed for the door, and she turned round when her hand was on the doorknob to inform him that she would be leaving first thing, whatever the weather.

'And no need for you to see us off,' she decided to tell him, to which he raised his eyebrows and kept looking at her until the colour crawled into her cheeks. 'We'll let ourselves out,' she finished lamely. Face flaming, Abigail dashed out of the kitchen, headed straight to the bedroom she had been allocated and only allowed herself to relax when that bedroom door was well and truly locked behind her.

She woke to the sound of knocking on her bedroom door, and when she sat up she realised with some dismay that it was after eight-thirty. She had planned to be up and out before seven. So much for that.

There was no service on her phone. It seemed that service was only available here and there in the house and her bedroom was not in that category. Still, she had texted the situation to Claire from downstairs the evening before, and could only hope that everything was all right. She was dying to get back to London.

The knocking continued. Abigail didn't have time to think about her state of undress. She'd had to sleep without anything on, because the alternative had been her work clothes, so she wrapped a bath towel round her and opened the bedroom door a crack to see Leandro outside, bright-eyed, bushy-tailed and looking unfairly drop-dead gorgeous in a pair of low-slung jeans and a thick cream jumper. She was conscious that the towel tightly wrapped round her barely skimmed her thighs.

He pushed the door open further with one foot and then folded his arms. 'I hate to wake Sleeping Beauty,' he said, eyeing the bank of windows behind her, across which the curtains had been tightly pulled, 'but I'm the bearer of bad tidings, I'm afraid…' Leandro watched with male appreciation at the enchanting picture Abigail made as she bolted towards the windows and yanked back the curtains with one hand while the other kept a tight hold on the towel.

She'd blown him off but there was no way he had any intention of retreating humbly to the sidelines to lick his wounds. That wasn't his style. He'd already determined the reason behind his malaise ever since they had broken up and he intended to do something about that. It would just take slightly longer and require slightly more thought than he had originally imagined.

For instance, he had optimistically harboured the assumption that one wild night in the hay would do the trick. So she'd knocked him back but, even if she hadn't, he could see that one night might not be enough to get her out of his system.

He'd somehow managed to forget the effect she could have on his libido. He was supremely confident about winning her over to his way of thinking because he had proved that she was still as turned on by him as he was by her. He was already gearing up for the thrill of that challenge as he heard her utter a soft exclamation of anguish as she saw that the snow, which should have gone away, hadn't. Out here, in the countryside, there were no gritted roads to give the illusion of things being done to remedy the situation either. The open fields that surrounded his palatial country manor were white and untouched. Not a gritting tractor in sight.

Abigail spun round to find that Leandro had entered the bedroom and was standing right behind her, and she jumped back and looked up at him. Their eyes tangled and for a few seconds she recalled what it had felt like to have him down between her thighs, bringing her to an orgasm that had been as devastating to her peace of mind as a runaway train mounting a crowded pavement. Dampness pooled between her legs, shocking and embarrassing.

'And it's only going to get worse.' He didn't bother

to try and soothe her into any positive thoughts on that score. 'Out here, the snow can last for days. That's why I seldom risk coming here in winter. What I'm saying here is that there's no way the car that brought you here can take you back. In fact, if you turn around and angle your body to the left, you can just about make out the shape of it semi-buried under white. Hal's been out to have a go at it and he managed to drive it a few metres before giving up. I doubt he could even get the thing out of my drive, and it's miles from here before you're lucky enough to hit any kind of road that might have been salted.'

'No, don't say that,' was all Abigail could find to respond, aghast at this development. 'You don't understand, Leandro. I *have* to get back to London.'

'I've talked to your driver and he's more than happy to wait it out here, which will in all likelihood be for another night. I shall ensure that he is fed and watered. Between us, I get the impression that the man sees this as a weekend break from a household of tetchy kids.'

'I don't *care* about whether Hal is willing to stay another night here!'

'Well, you should,' Leandro pointed out, 'considering he's your means of transport out. Unless you're insured on the car? But either way it's moot. The country roads will be impassable, anyway.'

Abigail wanted to sob. 'This is *all your fault*,' she

accused in a wobbly voice and Leandro shot her a perplexed look that further inflamed her because it reeked of insincerity.

'Explain,' he said drily. 'You must think I have superhuman powers if I can conjure up a fall of snow simply to scupper your plans for leaving. But, before you pull another "damsel in distress" fainting act, you'll be reassured to know that I have a similar problem. I, too, need to get down to London. Bear in mind that this weekend here was sprung on me as an unfortunate surprise. I hadn't planned on opening up the house until early spring.'

Abigail glumly wondered what that had to do with anything. So both of them would be stuck here. Little did he know that, whatever important deal he had to close, it was as nothing compared to the responsibilities she urgently had to return to.

'So what?' she said shortly.

'So you should go and change,' Leandro murmured.

Which was a sharp reminder to Abigail that she was still clutching a towel with absolutely nothing on underneath while he stood there, smirking.

She saw red and swallowed hard because this was not how she had envisaged her ring-bearing trip to the Cotswolds ending. Everything had gone wrong. The weather had been hideous. There had been no loving fiancée for the ring she had carefully transported. She had crashed into her past when she had least expected it. She had become a stupid victim of all those physical responses she knew she should have put behind her and, to top it off, meeting Leandro again out of the blue had forced her to confront all the decisions she had made in good faith.

And, as if all that wasn't bad enough, she was now going to be stuck here with him because fate couldn't do the decent thing and clear a path for her to return to London where she would have the peace and space to think things through.

'I will need to make some calls,' she muttered, and wanted to smack him very hard when he grinned at her.

'You're getting worked up over nothing,' he said in a placating voice that made her teeth snap together. 'Hal is going to be staying on another night because he will have to drive the car back down to London. Fortunately for you, there is alternative transport.'

'What do you mean?' Abigail frowned because, aside from skiing their way cross-country, she couldn't think of any other means of manoeuvring in the snowy conditions. And that wouldn't work because she had never been near a pair of skis in her entire life.

'I've had my guy fly my helicopter up this morning. I have a landing pad and, as long as the snow isn't too deep, it is always possible for me to get out if I need to.'

'You had your *guy* fly *your helicopter* up?'

'It's a luxury, I know,' Leandro imparted smugly.

'So…we're going to take a helicopter down to London?'

'Hence it's imperative that you slip out of your towel and get back into your working clothes.' He strolled towards the window and peered out before turning his attention back to her. 'The snow's fine but it's piling up fast. Leave it too long, and we really will be stranded here with Hal and an all-you-can-eat buffet of unused party food.'

Leandro truly felt that sometimes things happened for a reason and this snow was a perfect opportunity to deliver her back to London, minus her driver, and directly to her house, to discover exactly where that might be.

He felt extremely satisfied at being in control of the situation. He was particularly pleased because, the last time round, control had not been at his disposal and that had been a big mistake.

'Meet me in the hall in half an hour.' He headed for the door without looking back over his shoulder but in his mind's eye he could see her with that scanty towel trying hard to cover her up, and then he pictured her without it at all.

Naked and sexy and the stuff of all his fevered imaginings.

She'd had a night to think about...things. A night to realise that it would be futile to try and ignore the fire still burning between them. Her blushing and coy backing away had told its own story. She was as jumpy as a cat on a hot tin roof around him and he was convinced that, once she was in her own comfort zone, having been solicitously dropped off by him, she would relax and be open to exploring the chemistry between them.

Abigail watched Leandro shut the door behind him without a second glance back at her. Helicopter? That would make nothing of the trip and she would be back in her house within a couple of hours, if as long as that.

He would go his own way and she would really have to think about what happened next now that he had resurfaced in her life.

CHAPTER FOUR

ABIGAIL MANAGED TO find service on her mobile in the hall and she made a harried call to Claire while Leandro was outside, doing whatever had to be done to direct his pilot. She would be back within a couple of hours—so please could Claire hang on a little bit longer?

Hal was in the kitchen being fed. He couldn't have been happier at being left in the snowy Cotswolds, in a sprawling country mansion, with limitless supplies of wonderful food and drink. He would drive the car back down to London just as soon as the snow cleared.

By the time Leandro re-entered the house, she was a little more reassured that all was right on the home front and that there had been no problems with Sam. It was the first time she had ever left him overnight and she had been worried sick.

She was fidgeting to leave and Leandro looked at her curiously.

'How many more times are you going to look at your watch?' he drawled, cupping her elbow in his hand and propelling her towards the front door. He had already given his instructions to clean the house and then close it up until he could arrange to pay a return visit.

'I'm anxious, that's all. I've never been in a helicopter before.' Outside the snow continued to fall, the flakes small and sharp, the wind biting and instantly putting red into her cheeks. She hadn't banked on such severe weather and her trouser suit, even with her coat, felt like inadequate protection.

'Looking at your watch a hundred times isn't going to make you less anxious. Don't worry, you will be delivered to London safe and sound and in once piece.'

Ushered into the helicopter, a monstrous black beast that looked as though it could survive Arctic conditions, Abigail had some time to think as the machine roared into life, head-butting the lashing wind, and rising up and up.

'I'm sure I will be,' she said eventually, over the roar of the helicopter as it swung and made its way south. She risked a look at him and shivered because he was just so *dominant,* so incredibly overwhelming. He induced raw, forbidden excitement and dreadful, paralysing apprehension in equal measure. Since she had never thought to lay eyes on him again,

the apprehension was winning hands down just now
as the helicopter buzzed its rapid path away from the
snow towards cold, leaden skies that became clearer
the further south they travelled.

She had begun unhappily questioning the road she
had taken and the choices she had made and now,
as London drew closer and closer, she felt faint with
the sickening suspicion that she might have made the
wrong decision.

Abigail didn't want to think this way. She fought
to recover some of the conviction she had felt all
those months ago when she had decided not to contact Leandro.

She forced herself to remember that she had never
known her parents. She had no idea who her father
was because he wasn't even registered on her birth
certificate. Her mother was now only a vague memory because Abigail had been taken into care when
she had been just seven years old. She had known
little but the indifference of strangers who had been
paid to make sure that she was fed, watered and ed-
ucated in a manner of speaking.

The system in which she had grown up had made
her fiercely protective of her baby even before he
had been born.

That was why she had chosen to keep the pregnancy a secret, she reminded herself. She hadn't
dared risk Leandro, rich, powerful and filled with

hatred after the break-up of their relationship, trying to lay claim to his child. Of course, he might have chosen to walk away completely, given the option, or offer some financial support and nothing more, but that had been a risk she had been unwilling to take.

Who knew what the future held? she had asked herself. Maybe in time, when her baby was old enough to start asking questions, then she would reconsider the decision she had made, but by then she would be on her feet financially, would hopefully own her own house, and would certainly have many years of successful motherhood behind her to ensure that no one could take her child away from her.

In that manner, she had been able to shove any guilty conscience out of sight, and out of sight had been out of mind.

Her guilty conscience was certainly making up for lost time as she lapsed into silence during the short helicopter flight down to the outskirts of London.

The snow which had been falling steadily in the Cotswolds was not in evidence when they landed. It was cold and windy but, instead of snow, they exited the helicopter into freezing rain and Abigail wrapped her coat tightly around her and stood for a few seconds, getting her bearings.

'My car.' Hand propelling her gently behind her back, she found herself tripping along beside Leandro towards a gleaming black vehicle, at the side of which a smartly dressed middle-aged man was standing with the passenger door open.

With a stomach-churning feeling of someone on a rollercoaster ride, Abigail was deposited in the back seat of the car with Leandro next to her before she had time to consider what would happen next.

'Right.' Leandro slid shut a partition screen so that they were enclosed in complete privacy. 'Address?'

'Address?' She stared at him in alarmed silence as he waited patiently.

'Where do you live, Abigail?' He clicked his tongue impatiently as she continued to stare at him, cheeks a dull red, her mouth parted, her eyes wide. 'I need to tell my driver where to take you.'

Abigail closed her eyes briefly and rested her head against the leather seat. All the chickens had come home to roost now. She had closed the door on all those 'what if?' questions which foolishly she had been sure would never see the light of day.

What if Leandro discovered that he had a son?

What if she had chosen to tell him the moment she had discovered that she was pregnant?

What if he threatened to fight her for custody?

'You don't have to drop me to my house, Leandro,' she said with a touch of desperation. 'You can drop me to the shop. Vanessa will be keen to hear how the whole thing went. I tried emailing her yesterday but I don't think it was sent.'

'You're still in the same clothes from yesterday.'

'That doesn't matter. They're clean! And…and…'

'Just tell me where you live. I'm sure your boss can wait another hour for the urgent debrief.' He clearly wasn't going to take no for an answer.

Defeated, Abigail just looked at Leandro's bronzed, handsome face. She'd really and truly thought that she had put him behind her. She'd made a big mistake and fallen for someone utterly out of her league, and she had only discovered *just* how unreachable he was when he had believed his sister and the lies her ex-boss had told and refused even to allow her to give her side of the story.

She had fallen for a guy who had chosen to ignore everything they had shared because all he'd seen was a lying gold-digger who had used him. It hadn't mattered that they had done more than have sex. It hadn't mattered a jot that they had laughed, talked and done all the things that couples falling in love with one another do. Except, she had misread the signals. While *she* had been falling in love, *he* had just been having a bit of fun. All Leandro had shared with her was his body.

She'd been bitterly hurt and heartbroken when they had split up, but she'd had a lifetime of having to pull herself up and get on with things, and she had done it again. Her eyes had been opened and she had put him behind her as a mistake she had made.

One sidelong glance to her right was enough to confirm that she hadn't even come close to putting Leandro behind her. Her biggest mistake right now would be to let him see how vulnerable she still was as far as he was concerned.

She drew in a deep breath and said steadily, 'I think we need to talk before you drop me off at my house. Would you have some time? We could go to…a café close to where I live…'

Leandro leaned against the door and looked at her. Talking could only mean one thing and he controlled a kick of satisfaction at knowing what it meant. She'd had time to think about what he had said and the offer he'd put on the table was one that she was going to accept. Lust was a powerful thing and of course, he thought with cool rationality, there would also be the lure of money because she knew from experience that he was a generous man.

He smiled. 'I could spare the time,' he murmured. 'And we could always go to your place instead, or even mine. I have a place in Belgravia. Why don't I tell my driver to take us there and when we're finished…talking…he can drop you back to your flat? How does that sound?'

Abigail couldn't think of anything worse. As soon as she could, she would have to phone Claire and tell her to hang on for just a teeny bit longer, but there was no way she was going to his place in Belgravia, or anywhere else aside from a busy café, surrounded by people, where she would be able to say what she had to say and the fallout would be diluted. She knew very well why he'd want nothing more than for her to go to his house.

Not going to happen in a million years.

'No,' she said simply.

Leandro shrugged. He realised that he didn't care how much money he had to part with. He'd never wanted anyone the way he wanted her, and the fact that her CV as a woman who had lied to him and co-sied up to him under false pretences left a lot to be desired didn't seem to have diminished her appeal.

He was willing to throw the rule book out of the window just to get her out of his system once and for all. At least this time round he was in full possession of the facts and would be able to control the situation.

Abigail gave him the address of a café she had occasionally visited in the past and he dutifully relayed the information to his driver. Then—not because she was interested, but to break a silence that was beginning to make her skin prickle—she said, 'Your country house is magnificent, Leandro. How often do you get up there to stay?'

'A couple of times a year.' She had tied her hair

back once again but in his mind's eye he was seeing it in all its glory, hanging low down her back, vibrant and colourful. A few stray strands hung down on either side of her face and he wanted to tuck them neatly behind her ears and then pull her towards him so that he could feel the cool softness of her mouth on his.

'What a shame that you have so many houses in different parts of the world and you seldom get to enjoy them.'

'Perhaps, for me, it's the ownership that counts and that none of my properties will ever lose me money. I keep a sharp eye on them all and, over the years, they have done sterling work when it comes to increasing in value.'

'There's so much more to life than money.'

Leandro laughed shortly. 'Is this where we start going over old ground so that you can try and convince me that you're as pure as driven snow, despite the fact that you made no effort to tell me the truth about your background or about why, indeed, you were sitting in my hotel foyer in the first place?'

'No. I don't want to go over old ground any more than you do. I was just making small talk.'

'Feel free to skip the small talk.'

'If you dislike me so much, why do you still want to…sleep with me? How can you sleep with someone you dislike?'

'Do you have to ask that?' Leandro questioned roughly. 'Aren't we in the same boat? Driven by the same urges that haven't gone away? Or are you telling me that you have feelings for me? Because, if that's the case, then I should be clear right now and tell you that, sex or no sex, this is about wiping the slate clean and nothing more.'

Abigail resisted the urge to tell him that he was crazy if he thought that she wanted to talk to him because she had come round to his way of thinking, but then that would lead to all sorts of questions, and eventually to the conversation she knew would have to take place, but not in the back seat of his chauffeur-driven car.

'I don't have feelings for you, Leandro.' She stuck her chin out at a defiant angle. 'How could I?'

'Well, at least we're agreed on that score. I expect this conversation you want to have is to do with the terms and conditions of any liaison we enter into?'

'Yes, but not in the way you imagine,' Abigail told him truthfully.

Leandro shot her a half-smile. 'I'm a big boy, Abigail, and too experienced to be surprised by anything. Terms and conditions are a good thing in this situation.'

'Are they?' She was pretty sure that, firstly, he *wasn't* too experienced to be surprised by anything and, secondly, the terms and conditions she had in mind would take him so far out of his comfort zone that describing them as *a good thing* would be the last thing he'd do when she was done talking.

Done telling him what she'd never envisaged telling him. She should be scared stiff, but she felt very, very calm as the car continued to eat up the miles to the café. Sam was nearly one. She'd had months of motherhood and she felt much stronger than she had during those tumultuous months of pregnancy. Then afterwards, when she had held her new-born baby in her arms, she'd been torn between marvelling at the miracle of life looking at her with unfocused big, black eyes, and sickly wondering how on earth she was ever going to cope.

'Of course they are,' Leandro murmured, tilting her chin so that she was looking at him and actually *seeing* him instead of staring off into the distance, almost as if he no longer existed. 'I like terms and conditions. They're practical. They help keep things on an essential business level.'

Abigail's breathing quickened. His touch electrified her and that wasn't going to do. She wrested herself away but the blood had rushed into her face. 'If you'll give me a minute, I have to make a call before we get there.'

'We'll be there in under twenty minutes. What's the big rush?'

'I have a friend staying with me and I need to get in touch with her.'

'Friend? What friend?' His eyes narrowed and he shifted impatiently.

'My friend Claire is at home.' Abigail was already dialling. She'd planned to wait for a snatched moment when Leandro was otherwise occupied to make this call, but what did it matter now? Still, she kept the conversation brief, merely informing her friend that she would be home soon and thanking her for helping out.

'Helping out with what?' Leandro stared at her, frowning. Curiosity about her wasn't part of the deal and yet he was curious. Hushed conversations, he reasoned, had that effect on a person.

Abigail chose to ignore that because he would find out soon enough. 'I won't be able to hang around for long,' she said instead.

Leandro scowled at the brush-off but he decided to let it go. 'Nor will I,' he informed her. 'This whole sorry mess has screwed up my schedule. It might be Sunday but I've had to cancel several conference calls.'

Abigail felt a pang of sympathy for the woman who had now been reduced to the creator of a *sorry mess* that had put his work schedule out of sync.

She glanced through the window to find that they were already in North London, and it wasn't long before the car was pulling to a stop in front of the café, disgorging them both into damp cold and the onset of a fine, grey drizzle.

Her stomach clenched into knots as they found a table. She'd thought that it might have been busy but in fact the little chi-chi café, usually packed with yummy mummies or nannies with their little charges, was relatively empty.

'So…' Leandro wondered if she could look any more nervous. Should he help her out with the 'terms and conditions' chit-chat? Maybe ease the path by talking about his generosity as a lover? Clear the way for her to ask him what she wanted? Maybe not. 'Let's cut to the chase. Tell me what you wanted to talk to me about.'

They'd ordered coffees and these had now been brought to them, along with a selection of pastries, which she looked at without touching. He had no such qualms, breaking a croissant and looking at her steadily as he ate.

'Do you remember the time we went to that lake?'

Leandro paused mid-bite and gently replaced the croissant on his plate. He sat back, his big body loosely relaxed and yet tellingly still. He had no idea where this was going and that, in itself, wasn't working for him. He also didn't like the way she was fidgeting, playing with the rim of her cup and studiously avoiding his eyes.

'I remember,' he said abruptly. 'Five days in a little cabin by a lake just outside Toronto. Why do you ask? Trip down memory lane? I thought we'd agreed that there was no profit in going there.'

Abigail looked at him without any outward sign of the nervousness tearing her up inside. His lean, handsome face was closed and she knew that he would be annoyed because this was not what he had been expecting to hear. 'Something happened there, Leandro,' she said quietly. 'Do you remember?'

Leandro shook his head and raked his fingers impatiently through his hair. 'Are you going to carry on speaking in riddles, Abigail? Because I haven't come here to play guessing games with you.'

'We made love by the lake. Do you remember?' Her voice had grown wistful without her realising it. 'It was really warm and we'd been lying out on the jetty with a picnic lunch and a bottle of wine and we...we made love right there, out in the open.'

Leandro remembered it all. In fact, it had been the first time he had really felt as though he'd been on holiday, and he'd never felt so relaxed in his life before. Unfortunately, there was always a serpent lurking in paradise, and he wasn't going to be sucked into dwelling on a memory that didn't deserve an airing considering the revelations that had come later.

'We didn't use any contraception.'

Five little words dropped into the silence like unexploded bombs, except that it took a few seconds for them to sink in. She was looking at him carefully but his mind had gone blank and he felt like his thoughts were wrapped in fuzzy cotton wool.

'What are you saying?' he asked eventually.

'You know what I'm saying, Leandro.' Abigail's voice was gentle. 'I know you're probably going to be enraged, and maybe you'll think that I should have told you then, but I'm telling you now. We had unprotected sex and I got pregnant.'

'You're lying.'

'That's why I was so desperate to get back down to London. Claire, the friend I just spoke to, had agreed to look after Sam because I had to deliver the ring, but I never expected to get stuck up there.'

'If this is some sort of gimmick to get me to part with money, then you're overplaying your hand.'

They hadn't used any contraception. He'd been so turned on that he'd taken a risk. For the first time in his life, he had taken a risk.

'He's ten months old.'

'I refuse to believe a word of this.' But the burnished bronze of his golden skin was ashen. He *didn't* believe what she was saying, but he was still doing the maths.

She sighed. 'I would have told you right at the beginning, Leandro, but I was scared. We'd broken up under some pretty horrible conditions, and I was scared because I thought you might try and take Sam away from me.'

Leandro reached for his coffee cup and was surprised that his hand was unsteady.

'You need time to process all of this. I can see that.' Abigail stood up and began backing away from the table. 'If you let me have your mobile number, then I will give you a call in a couple of weeks' time, once you've…um…come to terms with…everything. And I just want you to know that I'm not expecting anything from you.'

The sight of her scuttling towards the exit galvanised Leandro faster than a rocket blazing into outer orbit. He slammed some money on the table and was by her side before she had time to do a runner.

Two weeks? Then she'd be in touch?

She'd just dropped a hand grenade into his lap and she really and truly thought that she could disappear and then resurface after he'd dealt with the fall out?

Had the woman lost her mind?

'Where the hell do you think you're going?' His hand circled her arm and he yanked her to a stop, ignoring her wriggling attempt to break free. 'Don't think that you can spring this on me and then vanish!'

'You need time to process…'

'Spare me your pop psychology! You tell me that you have a child…'

'*We* have a child. A son.'

Their eyes tangled. *A son.* There was no way that Leandro was going to cave in and believe her but... fatherhood. It was something he had never considered. Never wanted! He'd seen from his own unstable childhood that the production of children was something that could go horribly wrong. He'd not only learned from his own experience but he'd learned from his sister's. He'd never wished to reproduce and take a chance on being a father. It wasn't in his make-up.

What if she was telling the truth? Faced with that possibility, Leandro suddenly knew what it felt like for one's world to fall apart. He'd sought order all his life, to combat the lack of order that had marked his formative years, and there could be nothing more disastrous and explosive when it came to destroying all that hard-fought-for order than the arrival of a child.

But, no, he wasn't going to think like that.

He was a cool, rational man. He forced his thoughts away from *possibilities*. *Possibilities* counted for nothing.

'Where?'

'I beg your pardon?'

'You tell me that I'm a father. Then let me see my son.'

'Leandro...'

'This isn't going to play out the way you had in mind, Abigail. You don't get to spring something like this on me and then walk into the blue yonder. So you tell me that I have a son? Fine. Let's go and have a little meet and greet, shall we?'

He was clinging to this whole nonsense being a lie, but why would she lie about this? As fast as he tried to reason away the horror of what had been placed at his door, the counter-arguments piled up.

'I don't think—'

'No!' His voice cracked like a whip and she flinched and looked around her, but the street was quite empty of people. 'This situation is no longer within your control! You opened a door and now you can reap the consequences.'

Abigail stared at him, her eyes huge with dismay.

'Where do you live? And no beating about the bush, Abby. We go there and we go there *right now*, whether you like it or not.'

His car had been waiting on the other side of the road and Leandro hustled her towards it.

If his driver was in any way curious about the little sketch unfolding, he revealed nothing as he drove the ten minutes it took to get her to her house, a tiny rented place in a row of similar terraced houses.

Of course Claire would be agog. She had no idea that Sam's father was back on the scene because Abigail hadn't told her. But everything was happening so swiftly that this wasn't the time to launch into explanations.

But, as she hugged her friend and gently told her that *of course* everything was fine, she could practically inhale the scent of Claire's curiosity.

'Sam's asleep,' was the first thing she told Leandro, spinning round to look at him as soon as the front door was shut.

The house felt ridiculously tiny and his large, looming, threatening presence ate up the oxygen, making her light-headed with foreboding.

'I want to see him.'

'Do you still think I'm lying?'

'So, you have a son.' Leandro looked at her with flinty eyes. 'Who's to say that I am the father?'

'I would never lie to you about something like that.' She looked away because she didn't want to get into a squabble about the past and the lies he felt he had been told. Also, it hurt. It shouldn't, because he thought nothing of her now, but it still did. She blinked away an urge to cry. 'Follow me.' She spun round and he followed her as she made her way up the stairs to the little landing and to her bedroom, where Sam's cot was pushed up against the wall. It wasn't an ideal set up, but rents were high in London, and it was the best she could afford.

She always kept the side light by her bed switched

on. It was dim and it ensured that she didn't risk waking him up when she retired to bed for the night. The light was on now because the curtains had been drawn to block out the watery early-afternoon light.

It cast a mellow glow through the bedroom, which was as neat as a pin and done up in calm, neutral colours.

She stood back and Leandro walked towards the cot. He looked down.

He was so tall, so stunningly gorgeous, and she felt the sharp, piercing stab of real guilt that she had kept his son from him. Seeing him there, looking down into Samuel's cot, deprived her of all excuse for what she had done. A father looking down at his baby son. Sam was sleeping on his back, his short, chubby legs bent like a frog's at the knees, his arms raised on either side of his head.

Even in the dull, grey light the mop of dark hair and the faint olive of his skin was dramatic proof of paternity.

Staring into the cot, Leandro had no idea how much time passed by because it seemed to stand still. He'd looked out for his sister but he couldn't remember the time when she'd been as small as this.

Something filled him and he didn't know what it was. A vague, aching discomfort that was a nasty hollow in the pit of his stomach. The little boy had very dark hair like him, and he was olive-skinned, also like him. Clinging to the notion that he wasn't a father felt like a fantasy.

But he knew that he had to cling to it for a while longer. He would take nothing for granted. That just wasn't his nature and so he would not take this for granted even though somewhere deep inside he knew that the child was his.

And Abigail had kept him from him, would have *carried on* keeping him from him, had fate not forced their paths to cross.

Leandro had never thought about having children but now he was filled with the slow, steady pulse of rage that he'd been kept in the dark about the biggest thing that was possible to happen in anyone's life.

He turned away from the cot and looked at her, his face all angles and shadows. Then he moved towards her.

'Time…to talk.'

CHAPTER FIVE

'I'LL WANT A DNA TEST,' was the first thing Leandro said the second they were in her kitchen. He hadn't paid a scrap of attention to his surroundings, but now he did, and he didn't like what he saw. A small, shabby house hardly big enough to swing a cat in. Fresh paint and cheerful posters couldn't quite conceal the fact that the place was probably held together by masking tape and glue, and the rage that had swept through him earlier on, after he had looked down at the dark-haired baby in the cot, swept through him once again—a red tide that made him clench his jaw in an effort to exert some control.

There was still room for doubt.

Abigail was hardly noted for her fervent adherence to the truth. She'd spent weeks papering over her background and the small matter of the theft hanging over her head. She'd effectively lied to him, and right now he chose to disregard all the reasons she had come up with for her evasions. Right now he could only think that, if that baby upstairs was his, then life as he knew it was about to be turned on its head.

Abigail paled. 'You mean you don't believe me,' she said flatly.

'You come with a reputation. Taking you at your word would be a ludicrous act of charity on my part.' He pulled a chair and sat down, pushing it back so that he could extend his long legs. He felt like a giant in a playhouse.

The thought of any baby of his being raised in this sort of environment set his teeth on edge, and just like that he was shocked that his thoughts were already travelling down that road, already accepting possibilities.

One step at a time, he reminded himself grimly.

He would deal with the situation only when full paternity was revealed.

But the maths made sense…then there was that physical resemblance…and did he truly, in his heart, believe that she was the sort of woman who somehow would have thrown herself into bed with another man the second they'd parted company?

Leandro had a moment of complete terror, because suddenly he could see the ordered and well-oiled life he had built for himself falling apart at the seams.

'You're Sam's father, Leandro.' Abigail tilted her chin at a mutinous angle and held her ground but her world was shifting on its axis and she had no idea where it was going to end up. Right now, that look on his face was sending shivers of apprehension up and down her spine.

He'd wanted her for five minutes, wanted to have her back in his bed to *scratch an itch* until the itch went away. There had been no lingering affection behind that. Indeed, he had made sure to tell her that, so what on earth would he be thinking now?

Surely he must realise that a DNA test wasn't necessary? But then, Leandro's opinion of her was so low that he might actually believe that she would have disembarked at Heathrow airport over a year ago, broken-hearted, and headed for the nearest bar so that she could pick up a random stranger and drag him off to bed somewhere.

He loathed her, so where did that leave them? She should have been regretting bitterly the impulse to confess, but she wasn't. Seeing him standing over the cot and looking down into it had made her realise that she couldn't keep Sam from him. She had made her decision to say nothing for reasons that had been right for her at the time but, whatever the consequences now, it was right that he knew.

Which didn't help when it came to trying to figure out what happened next.

'I'm not asking for anything from you,' she said quietly. 'You didn't ask for this situation and you don't have to think that your life is going to be messed up because of it.' She'd sat opposite him and she was very much aware of how tiny the kitchen was because he took up so much space in it. In fact, she was very much aware, ever since he had entered the house, of how confined her surroundings were. Her heart began a slow, scared drum roll inside her chest.

If *she* could see the limitations of where she lived, and she'd grown accustomed to it over the months, then what must *he* be seeing?

This was a man with a helicopter and flash properties worth millions scattered across the globe. He snapped his fingers and everyone around him jumped to attention. A house wouldn't be a house for him unless every bedroom came with an *en suite* bathroom and a separate dressing room.

He was going to get a stupid DNA test, which would come back positive, and what then? Would he want to rescue his son from these surroundings? He couldn't. The sensible side of her saw that, because mothers had rights too, but he could provide so much as Sam's father and he could fight her with all the time and money at his disposal if he felt so inclined.

It suddenly seemed imperative that she persuade him that having his life remain as it was was what he wanted and needed.

'It was an honest mistake.' She smiled reassuringly at him. She felt about as sincere as the wicked witch smiling at Hansel and Gretel while she tried to lure them into the gingerbread house. 'You didn't ask for a child, Leandro, and I know what your life-style's like. Your feet hardly ever touch the ground! You said yourself that you rarely get to visit your beautiful country house. I'll bet you're hardly ever in England at all!'

She cleared her throat and wished that he would say something. Agree with her, preferably. Or at least give some indication that he was hearing what she was saying. He was looking at her with brooding intensity and it was doing nothing at all for her equilibrium. Or for the sensible, rational part of her that *knew* he couldn't sweep in and carry Sam off with him just because he was rich.

'What I'm saying,' she finished with a lot more bracing confidence than she was feeling, 'Is that I wouldn't want you to stop living the life you're living because of this. I'm perfectly capable of bringing Sam up on my own.'

'I will make arrangements for a paternity test.'

'Is that all you can say, Leandro?'

'What would you like me to say?' His voice was deathly quiet. 'That if you're right, and he's my son, that I'll oblige you by disappearing because it was all an *honest mistake*?' He stood up and looked down at her. 'I have no intention of taking your word for anything,' he said calmly. 'I'm a very rich man and whether I believe what you're telling me or not makes no difference. I am an easy target for gold-diggers.'

'I'm not a gold-digger, Leandro, and you should know that.'

Leandro's heart clenched at the genuine hurt in her face but he wasn't going to retract a word of what he'd said. He'd been invigorated by the thought of pursuing her to take her to his bed so that he could finish something that had been started, something that needed a proper conclusion so that he could get on with his life, but now things had changed. Very, very dramatically.

'What will the procedure be?' she asked, defeated. 'Will Sam have to go to a hospital for the test?'

'It will be handled discreetly. You will hear from me tomorrow about arrangements for the test and once the results are known...' He looked at her narrowly and thought about the small, softly breathing shape in the cot. Something threatened to engulf him, a depth charge as powerful as an earthquake. 'We will take it from there.'

'Leandro...' She stepped towards him then hesitated and remained where she was, hovering and uncertain.

'I'll be in touch.'

He didn't get in touch, but by lunchtime the following day she was contacted by a consultant employed by him to perform the test, and by six that evening the technician had come and gone and she had received a call from Leandro informing her that he, too, had been tested in accordance with the paternity-test requirements.

If Abigail had been hoping for some kind of clue as to what he was thinking underneath the clipped voice and the curt words, then she'd been barking up the wrong tree. The conversation, the first she'd had with him since he'd left her house, lasted ten seconds.

But the DNA test results would take at least a week, when you factored in overworked and underpaid health service workers who couldn't jump to attention and put their particular kit to the top of the queue. A week of breathing space. It would give her time to plan ahead for all possible eventualities.

She hadn't been expecting to see Leandro three days after he had left her house, and she certainly hadn't been expecting him to show up at the shop in all his dark, avenging glory.

About to leave for the day, Abigail looked up and there he was, standing in the doorway, a tall, commanding presence that made her breath hitch in her throat and set up a nervous drum beat in her chest.

Everyone in the shop instantly stopped what they'd been doing. Two customers fell silent and stared. Brian, who worked alongside her, gaped. A woman, who looked no older than twenty-one and was dripping in jewellery, started breathing far more quickly than could be deemed healthy. Leandro ignored them all. He strolled towards her, face cool, expression unreadable.

Like a rabbit caught in the headlights, Abigail was finding it a challenge to move a muscle. In fact, she was finding it a challenge to breathe as he continued to close the distance between them.

'The results are back.'

She blinked and unfroze. 'I… I thought you said that you were going to call me.'

'I thought that breaking the news face to face would be a far better idea. We need to talk, Abigail, and unless you want us to have this conversation here then you're going to make your excuses and leave.'

'But I'm not due to finish for another two hours!'

'I don't care if you've just stepped through the door to start your day.' He looked around him, caught Brian's eye and turned back to her. 'That the guy in charge?'

'Give me five minutes… And, please, could you wait outside?'

'I'm very comfortable here.'

Abigail glared but had a hurried, low-key conversation with Brian and within minutes they were outside, back in the freezing February cold.

'My car is over there.' Leandro nodded towards the black chauffeur-driven car. 'Here's what we're going to do. We're going to go to my apartment—which is twenty minutes away—we are going to have a civilised conversation, and then we are going to go and get my son from whatever day-care place you've stuck him in.'

'You can't order me around.' But Abigail heard the weakness in her voice that signalled capitulation.

'You should be glad I've decided to go down the civilised route, Abigail. Because, right now, the last thing I feel is *civilised*.'

'Look…' She turned to him as the car into which she had been channelled like a kidnap victim pulled away, 'I can understand that you might be a little… annoyed…'

'A *little annoyed*?' Leandro looked at her with scathing disbelief. She was wearing practically the same drab outfit she'd been wearing when she had crash-landed back into his life days before. Her hair was tightly pulled back and her face was bare of all but minimal make-up. She looked like a mid-level career woman. Neither in her demeanour nor in her svelte shape did she betray any signs of being a mother. There was no way he could ever have guessed that she was, and again it hit him like a sledgehammer that she had kept his son from him.

She'd given him a way out with her speech about not wanting anything from him and, although he had never contemplated fatherhood, that 'way out' had struck him as offensive and insulting. His reaction had surprised him in its ferocity, as had the surge of primitive emotion that had gripped him when he had slit open that hand-delivered report to discover what he had known all along: the chances of him being Sam's father were ninety-nine per cent.

'What gave you the right to withhold my son from me?' Leandro gritted. 'Did you think that because we had broken up I was no longer due the decency of being told that I had fathered a child?'

Abigail flushed. For a man who was so good at keeping his emotions in check, those few words were incendiary.

They fired her up into a burning anger that matched his. What gave him the right to lay into her? They hadn't just *broken up.* He had rid himself of her the way someone would rid themselves of vermin. He had dispatched her as a criminal and a liar and now had the barefaced nerve to accuse her of lacking the *decency* to tell him that she had been pregnant!

'Start as you mean to go on' was the saying that sprang to mind, and Abigail suspected that, if she started by lying down and becoming a doormat he felt free to walk all over, then that would be her role forever, whatever joint way forward they finally found.

'I wasn't exactly filled with confidence that, if

I threw myself at your feet and told you that I was pregnant, you wouldn't do your best to hurt me for all that stuff you'd been told by your sister!'

'The truth, you mean?'

'There you go! It was over three months after we broke up before I even found out that I was pregnant. I was so anxious about my future, so desperate to get a job, so worried about where I would end up living because all my savings were running out, that I didn't even notice that my periods had stopped! And, yes, I suppose I *could* have come running to you for help, but guess what? When you're accused of being a liar and a thief and a gold-digger, the last thing that occurs to you in a moment of blind panic is to turn to your accuser for help.'

'I wasn't just a random ex-boyfriend.' Leandro wasn't going to let her get away with that, 'I was the man who'd fathered the child you were carrying.'

He sighed with frustrated impatience and bit down hard on the bitter recriminations that begged to find a way out. They would be at his apartment in under five minutes. He'd drawn the partition and his driver couldn't hear a word they were saying but he still felt that he needed her somewhere entirely private in which to have this life-changing conversation. The back of a car just wasn't working for him.

'I told you,' Abigail reminded him in a driven voice, 'I was scared. Scared that you would try and take him away from me—that I would never be able to fight you, because you're rich and powerful, and at the time I was jobless and virtually unemployable, thanks to that scumbag of an ex-boss who'd lied about me.'

'What makes you think that I won't try and do that now?' Leandro asked.

Abigail froze and looked at him with horror. 'You wouldn't dare!'

'It's always a mistake to lay down a challenge to a man like me.' Leandro let the silence stretch between them, interminably long. Why not let her imagination go wild? It was the very least she deserved, as far as he was concerned.

'We're here. We can continue this conversation inside.'

Abigail, who could hardly think for the blind panic racing through her, and the worst-case scenarios filling her head, glanced distractedly at the elegant white building in front of which the car was slowing. Precise, black wrought-iron railings enhanced the windows, which were perfectly spaced and perfectly rectangular—like a child's drawing of what the outside of a house should look like, with all the dimensions of ruler-like precision. They entered a large hallway, tiled in original Victorian tiles, and were whooshed up in silence in the lift to his apartment, which she found extended over two floors and was as big as a house.

It was all white, aside from the dramatic, abstract works of art on the walls. The floor was blonde wood. There were no curtains at all, just shutters. The staircase that wound up to a galleried landing was the least child-friendly item of house décor she had ever seen in her entire life. Metal and with a token safety railing that would encourage any adventurous toddler to fall under. She was horrified.

Leandro was watching her carefully, and he frowned, because his apartment never failed to impress. He'd employed the best interior designer in London who had sourced materials from across Europe to create the perfect place. No expense had been spared and that was obvious, from the rich grey granite in the open-plan kitchen, to the pale wood on the floor which had been specially flown in from The Netherlands at great cost. Half of the paintings were by iconic and recognisable artists, the other half were investment pieces by up-and-coming artists, and their value increased weekly. The furniture was all bespoke.

'What's wrong?' he asked irritably and Abigail swivelled round to look at him, her hands belligerently folded.

'I hate this apartment,' she said bluntly, spreading one arm wide in a gesture of dismissal that got on his nerves.

'Don't be crazy. Of course you don't. No one hates this apartment.'

'It's…it's…soulless…cold. A *mausoleum* would have more atmosphere!'

Leandro glowered and remembered that she had never been shy about speaking her mind. In fact, she'd been the only woman in living memory ever to have disagreed with him about anything and he'd enjoyed it. She'd always been magnificent when she was arguing. She looked bloody magnificent now. He stared at her in brooding silence, noting the hectic flush in her cheeks, the pinkness of her full mouth and the fiery glitter in her bright green eyes.

Faster than a speeding bullet, his body responded to her with shocking enthusiasm. He hardened and his desire increased. Disgusted with himself, Leandro turned away and headed for one of the cream sofas artfully arranged around the only rug in the apartment, a grey hand-woven affair with a bold white, abstract pattern.

'Speaking of residences,' he told her coldly, 'let's move away from the shocking condition of mine and let's talk about yours. When you were thinking about yourself and making your far-reaching decision to exclude me from my son's life, did you ever stop to think that he might have benefited from the financial support I would have been able to give? That, instead of condemning him to a house the size of a matchbox, his life may very well have been improved by being somewhere bigger? Understood, at the age of ten months it's not that urgent, but what when he begins to crawl? To walk around? Were you so busy being selfish that you managed to happily justify denying him all the advantages my money could have brought to the situation?'

Abigail flushed, dismayed at being labelled selfish, yet seeing it from his point of view and not at all liking the picture he was painting of her.

'And what about,' Leandro continued mercilessly, 'when my son got old enough to start wondering where his father was?'

'Stop referring to Sam as *your* son. He's *our* son.' Warmth spread through her because, unwittingly, she had joined them up, voiced what she had denied for the past year and a half: that she wasn't the only parent involved in this equation. She'd pretended that she was, but that was no longer the case, and she thought uneasily that perhaps it shouldn't have been the case at all. Not that she was going to start apologising for anything.

Leandro didn't miss that slip of the tongue and was quietly pleased because it showed that she was no longer fighting him. It didn't make it any easier to stomach what she had done but, in truth, he could almost see her point of view. He *had* walked away without giving her the chance to defend herself. He had taken his sister at her word and had refused to see that the woman he'd been sleeping with, the woman he'd felt he'd known, might have had her reasons for not being quite as open with him as she could have been. He'd reached conclusions and he had thrown those conclusions at her and, yes, they'd pretty much added up to her being a thief, a liar and, by extension, a gold-digger.

Well, if time had proved one thing, it was this. She was no gold-digger or else she would have landed on his doorstep within seconds of finding out that she was pregnant. She wouldn't have avoided him, she would actively have sought him out, because— he had to face it—she would have been holding the ultimate trump card.

She was telling the truth when she said that she'd been scared and he knew why—because he was ruthless. She'd been terrified of him trying to take her child away from her, and she'd had good cause to be apprehensive because of the way they'd broken up. And not just that, he was forced to concede with searing honesty—he had always made it clear to her that he wasn't interested in commitment, even though he had come uncomfortably close to revising that decision during the time he'd been with her. He grudgingly admitted to himself for the first time that this was possibly why he had rushed to believe Cecilia, but had rushed to break off the relationship with Abigail, a relationship that had come way too close to challenging his long-held beliefs.

He thought of her alone—scared, broke and dealing with a momentous situation on her own.

Had there even been anyone by her side when she'd delivered Sam? Or had she got herself off to hospital on her own?

'I *did* think about what might happen when Sam was old enough to start being curious,' Abigail muttered uncomfortably.

'And what conclusions had you come to?' Disconcerted by the introspective route his thoughts had taken him, Leandro's tone was sharper and cooler than he'd intended. 'Had you decided that you'd write off my existence on a permanent basis to make life easier for you? "Lost at sea" or something like that?'

'No!' Abigail was horrified that he could come to such a conclusion. Was he being serious? 'I would never, ever have done anything like that!' She found that she couldn't bear the thought of anything happening to him. Indeed, she felt physically ill at the thought.

His tone softened at the distraught expression on her face. From old, he knew that her fire was counterbalanced by a real capacity for empathy.

How was it that he hadn't seen that at the time, when he had walked out on her without a backward glance?

'You need to think past yourself,' he urged, leaning forward, forearms resting on his thighs, all his leashed power at bay but ferocious intent still stamped on his lean, beautiful face. 'Think about what Sam will think if years down the road he believes that you deprived him of a lifestyle that could have been within his reach.'

'What are you talking about?' Abigail frowned in confusion at this new angle he'd decided to explore.

'Don't you think that if you wait until he's a teenager, demanding to know who I am, that one look at the privileges that have passed him by might lead to a certain amount of resentment?'

'I would never raise any child of mine to be materialistic,' Abigail countered gamely, while her mind took hold of this whole new disturbing slant and began to chew it over.

'That's as may be,' Leandro continued remorselessly, 'but, human nature being what it is, unless you manage to raise a saint he will look at what could have been his and sooner or later blame you for denying him the opportunities that could have been at his disposal.' He allowed a few seconds of silence so that she could mull over this scenario in her head.

He knew that he was battering her from all sides, and he quelled his guilt, because guilt was the last thing he should be feeling. The truth was that he meant to see this through to its inevitable conclusion and he was determined to get the result he wanted whether she liked it or not. She was just going to have to see past herself and absorb the bigger picture, so painting all the potential minefields that awaited her should she not come round to his point of view was necessary. Simple as that, because all was fair in love and war.

'Unless,' Leandro mused thoughtfully, 'you plan on scaling the dizzy heights of financial success.'

'I hate you.' She glared at him and he raised his eyebrows in response.

'You hate what I'm telling you, but you have to hear it, because we're in a situation that requires a solution—and before we can reach that solution it's important for you to stand back and look at everything from all possible angles.'

'How can you be so…so…*unemotional* at a time like this?'

'Aren't you pleased that I am? What's the alternative? That I sit here sobbing and wringing my hands in despair?'

His wry humour leapt out at her, almost but not quite making her want to smile. Why couldn't he just be a complete bastard instead of reminding her that there was so much more to him? Right now, the last thing she wanted was to see the complex guy she had fallen in love with, the guy who could be as clever as the devil and as funny as any stand-up comedian. She didn't want three-dimensional.

Agitated, she sprang to her feet and began pacing.

She glanced at everything around her, at the opulence dripping from every surface.

'My house may be tiny but this apartment is ridiculous when you think about putting a child in it!' she burst out accusingly, moving to stand directly in front of him with her hands on her hips, then immediately wishing that she hadn't because the powerful effect of his personality made her giddy.

'I appreciate your honesty,' he said gravely and she glared at him.

'No, you don't,' she snapped. 'I don't suppose you've ever welcomed anyone being *honest* with you.'

'Wrong. You were honest with me about some things when we were together. I distinctly remember you telling me that I lived in an ivory tower, and then taking it upon yourself to introduce me to the fun of fast-food dining. You called me a show-off who liked to flash my money around and laughed because I was outraged.'

A wave of colour flooded her cheeks and she stared at him, taken back in time for a few seconds, amazed that he remembered that incident—when he'd obviously never really been attached to her the way she'd been attached to him because it hadn't taken him two minutes to find her replacement.

Flustered, she bought herself some time by continuing to glare at him. 'Everything in here is white.' She looked pointedly at the off-white sofa on which he was sprawled. 'A toddler would wreak havoc with all your furniture, and that excuse of a handrail...' she glanced behind her to the culprit before returning her triumphant gaze to his admittedly unfazed face '...well, that's an accident waiting to happen.'

'So you've decided that eliminating me from the picture isn't going to do. Good. We're on the same page with that.'

Abigail sat back down. She guessed that this was where the conversation would really begin, the starting point for making arrangements for visiting or whatever. She was staring at a future in which he would be part of her life for evermore, two people on parallel tracks joined together by the child they'd produced. Rattled, she gulped and stared at him.

'I guess we can sort out visiting rights,' she conceded faintly. 'Would you want me to sign something? And, if you want to contribute financially, then that would be fine.' She drew in a deep breath as she remembered that vague threat he had issued earlier. 'But there's no way I would ever let you try and take Sam away from me.' Abigail found her courage and met his eyes without blinking.

'I wouldn't dream of it,' Leandro assured her.

'You said...'

'I advised you to contemplate the option.' He looked at her thoughtfully. 'Here's the thing...' he murmured in a soft, low voice that made her shiver and did weird but idiotically predictable things to her nervous system. 'You're right about my apartment.' He sat back and gestured to the expanse of pristine white surrounding them without taking his eyes from her face. 'Not user-friendly when it comes to children, and you can work on changing that.'

'I beg your pardon?'

'Think of it as a blank canvas, and do whatever you want to bring it up to scratch.'

'I'm not following you…'

'And then, when you've got it exactly as you want it,' he continued into the bewildered silence, 'we can set about hunting for somewhere outside London— but not as distant as my Cotswolds place. In fact, I have had several people champing at the bit to get their hands on Greyling. I might just give one of them what they want and then we can search for somewhere more commutable. What are your thoughts on Berkshire?'

'I'm not following you, Leandro!'

'Of course you are,' Leandro said silkily. 'We have a child, and I'm not going to get embroiled in visiting rights and custody battles. I never thought about fatherhood but, now that it's appeared from a great height, I intend to deal with it in the most logical manner possible. A child deserves both parents and the stability of a unified background.'

He sighed heavily and sifted his fingers through

his hair. 'My parents were married,' he informed her quietly, 'but that's where the unity stopped—and you should know exactly what I'm talking about. We have a child between us, whether it was planned or not, and I intend to make sure that our child is brought up with both of us present, in a stable atmosphere. Nothing less is going to do.'

'So you're saying…'

'Marriage, Abigail. Like it or not, there's no other way.'

CHAPTER SIX

'NO OTHER WAY?' Abigail parroted, shock writ large all over her face. She had gone through a million and one scenarios of what could happen ever since she had told Leandro about Sam, but a marriage proposal hadn't featured in any of those scenarios.

'Correct. As I've made clear, I'm not going to subject our son to a back-and-forth situation between us.'

'Leandro, we can't *get married.*' Her voice had gone up a couple of octaves and was bordering on hysterical. She swallowed and breathed deeply, in and out, slowly and evenly, counting to ten, because approaching this situation with ranting was going to settle her firmly on the back foot before their negotiations had even begun. 'In an ideal world, a child is a cherished addition to the family unit and is blessed with two loving parents, but it's not an ideal world. Telling me that that's what we would be providing for Sam if we got married is just…just a *fantasy.*'

Leandro flushed darkly. He had offered to make the greatest sacrifice he knew for the sake of their child and he was incensed that she could throw his proposal back in his face without bothering to think things through. Buried beneath his anger was also a certain amount of pique. Countless women would have bitten his hand off for the proposal she was self-righteously tossing aside.

'Since when is it a fantasy to want the best for a child?'

'It's not,' Abigail told him in a long-suffering voice that really got on his nerves. 'Marriage is just not necessary in this day and age.' She jumped up and once again began pacing through the gloriously all-white room. Just looking around her was enough to show her how great the differences were between them. They were chalk and cheese, and it was no wonder his sister had been appalled when she had found out about their relationship. When he had turned his back on her, she had been left in his flash penthouse apartment in New York to pack her things and clear off, and she had had the pleasure of listening to his sister rant about her unsuitability for her brother.

'Leandro needs someone of his own class,' Cecilia had stormed, while Abigail had packed her bag in frozen silence, too distressed with Leandro's disappearance really to pay much attention to what Cecilia had been telling her. 'You're no good for him. He can't get involved with a thief, and it's just a good thing that I had the wit to get involved and rake up that stuff about you or else heaven only knows what might have happened!'

Nothing would have happened, as it turned out. The fact that Leandro had found it so easy to walk away had said it all. Now, here he was proposing marriage, but she was still the same person who was unsuitable for him, the same person he had found it easy to walk away from.

'I'm willing to let you see Sam whenever you want to,' she told him. 'And I get it that you can give him opportunities that I would never be able to in a million years, so of course if you want to contribute financially then I have no problem with that. But it would be a complete disaster for us to get involved in any other way. I mean, the world is full of kids who grow up perfectly happily when their parents are divorced or separated.'

'I don't care about those cheerful kids you tell me thrive when their parents are separated,' Leandro said calmly.

'Why won't you *listen* to me?' Abigail burst out. 'We don't come from the same world,' she enunciated in a low, urgent voice. 'It would never work. Your sister was right about that. I'm from a different class and never the twain shall meet. At least, not unless you want to become infected by me. So, marriage? It wouldn't last five seconds, and a break-up would be worse for a child than two adults who can communicate in a friendly fashion but aren't saddled with one another.'

'Rewind.' Leandro was frowning. 'What are you talking about?'

'It would end in tears, Leandro. You can't stick two people together who don't like one another and hope it works out for the sake of a child, especially when that child is the result of an accident.'

'What did Cecilia say to you?'

'What?' Perplexed, Abigail stared at him. It was always dangerous doing that because she found that, once she started looking, she couldn't stop and it was no different now, even though they were in the middle of a heated argument. Or, at least, she was. Leandro was so assured, so controlled, so stupidly beautiful. It was no wonder she had fallen head over heels in love with him and it was no wonder that even now, when the love bit had crashed and burned, her body still responded to that dark, powerful magnetism in ways that left her feeling addled and all at sea.

'I admit that there was no need for Cecilia to ride in to my rescue.' Leandro grimaced because his habit of indulging his sister had never left him, even though now he could see that she was wilful, where once that could have been interpreted as restless and youthfully energetic. 'But she did it with the best of intentions.'

Abigail couldn't help herself. She rolled her eyes, gritted her teeth and clenched one fist because for a guy who was so clued in he could be shockingly *stupid*.

Momentarily distracted, Leandro frowned. 'She's protective of me.' He gritted his teeth. 'It comes with the territory. I effectively looked after her because our parents were too busy pretending that they didn't have to grow up.'

'Cecilia isn't protective,' Abigail said in a rush. 'She's possessive and it's not healthy. Okay..' she was constrained to be fair '…she might be protective, and she might have been anxious that you'd get wrapped up with someone who might have been after your money, but that's not the only reason she was determined to break us up. Cecilia didn't think that I was good enough for you and she made that perfectly clear once you were out of earshot. "A common little tramp who should go back to the dustbin she crawled out of" was how she put it!' She sighed and sat down, spreading her fingers flat on her lap and staring down at them. She felt mean talking about his sister when she wasn't there to defend herself but why shouldn't Leandro know what she thought? Their class differences were just another thing to take into account, whether he liked it or not.

'Cecilia and I are not as close as we once were,' Leandro murmured reflectively. Had he been too generous in forgiving a side to his sister that it had been easier to ignore than acknowledge? He thought back to Cecilia's enthusiasm when he had taken the bait and started going out with Rosalind, the perfect mate on paper with the right pedigree and all the right credentials.

'I apologise for having said anything, Leandro,' Abigail told him stiltedly, 'but Cecilia had a point. We don't come from the same background.'

'We're getting off topic here.' He would think about his sister later. He'd taken his eye off the ball with her, and maybe it was time to correct that oversight, but right now there were more important things to focus on.

'We're not. I'm just trying to make you see why this marriage proposal of yours doesn't make sense.'

He looked at her, his brilliant eyes veiled. 'I am not prepared for you to have another man in your life,' he said bluntly, 'who will inevitably have influence over my son.'

Abigail laughed because it seemed ludicrous for him to be thinking about another man in her life. She hadn't so much as glanced at anyone since Leandro and she drew a blank when she thought about moving on and doing normal stuff like going on dates and getting to know other men.

Who could possibly ever compare to him? Reluctantly, she looked at him and did a quick mental comparison between Leandro and every other single man she had ever spoken to, communicated with or even set eyes on in her entire life.

Leandro won hands down, and it wasn't just because of the way he looked. He was larger than life in his dynamism, his vitality, his overpowering sexual magnetism. She had sensed that the very second he had approached her in that hotel foyer and she had allowed herself to go with the flow. Only afterwards had she worked out that a man like Leandro could have any woman and that the relationship that had become more and more significant for her had, for him, remained firmly on the same footing on which it had begun.

'How do you feel about another *woman* in *my* life?' he asked shrewdly, and Abigail snapped out of the wistful reverie that had swept over her. She blinked, focused and thought about what he had said.

Wasn't it far more likely that he would be snapped up? Women with a child in tow were never seen as sex sirens and, on a practical level, Abigail knew that she would struggle to find the time to go out and paint the town red anyway. She would carry on with her job, because she would want to maintain her independence, and between her job and looking after Sam—even if there *was* an injection of cash that made things easier—her life would be as hectic as it always was.

But a man with an infant in tow, a *sexy, eligible billionaire bachelor with an infant in tow,* would be even more of a catch because there was nothing sexier than a guy pushing a pram. Leandro wouldn't even have to try. He would be targeted and there would be another Rosalind out there who would snap him up sooner rather than later. Chances were that, with a child to consider, he would be far more amenable to the concept of getting married. Subconsciously, he would be seeking out a mate with whom he would be able to share parental duties.

How would she feel about that?

She broke out in tingly perspiration. Of course this was what sharing a child was all about, she told herself stoutly. Blended families. It happened every day of the week!

Unfortunately, thinking about a blended family with Leandro in the starring role, and some gorgeous, upper-class blonde as his co-star, made her feel sick.

She started when he suddenly stood up and looked at his watch. 'What time do you collect Sam?'

Dazed, Abigail looked at him and blinked like an owl. 'Not for another couple of hours,' she admitted.

'You put him in childcare every day, nine to six?'

She bristled and followed him to the kitchen,

where he began rummaging in a cupboard, fetching the ingredients for coffee. 'Vanessa is very generous with my hours,' she told him. 'I get in at nine-thirty and work until four and I have Fridays off. I usually catch up with whatever admin is outstanding then. She understands the pressures on working mothers. Not many employers do.'

Abigail's mind was still furiously playing with the image of a Leandro all settled down with a woman, a woman actually destined to wear the engagement ring he had kept for investment purposes. Wasn't it fair to say that she would resent some other woman holding Sam? Cooing at him? Pushing him on a swing in the park?

Would she be laughing up at Leandro, holding his hand and planning the perfect little family holiday with Sam...?

'I don't approve of my son being stuck in a nursery for hours on end.' Leandro delivered this on a note of finality. 'Do you? Honestly?'

Abigail hesitated and then blurted out defensively, 'What choice did I have? I had to get out there and earn a living to keep the roof over our heads.'

'And yet you never thought to seek me out and ask for help.'

'No. Not once,' she said honestly.

'You must have been lonely,' Leandro suddenly commented, surprising himself and her with the incisive remark, and Abigail blushed and hesitated. Without her noticing, he'd brought her coffee, and oddly he'd remembered how she took it—strong with very little milk.

'I got through it,' she said, tilting her chin at a bullish angle and leading him to think of her as a kid out there looking after herself, doing whatever it took to put one foot in front of the other. Which made him think of the shoplifting charge against her, and he had a sudden wave of sympathy for her youthful desire to fit in.

'So you did.' He looked at her reflectively until she went bright red and began to toy with the handle of the mug. 'I'm making this sound like a business deal,' he drawled, and Abigail flicked a glance at his lean, thoughtful, outrageously handsome face.

'Isn't it?' she questioned. 'You've found out that you have a child and…and… I'm *sorry* that I didn't tell you at the time. Perhaps I should have but, at the time, keeping it to myself felt like the right thing to do.' Abigail sighed and absently curled one long, escaped strand of hair round her finger, then undid the little bun and smoothed her hand through its long mass, before propping her chin in the palm of her hand and staring at him. 'And now you're approaching the *problem*—and, yes, that's what you called it, Leandro—with the most logical solution you can think of that fits in with your desire to be a full-time father, now that you've been put in the position of having to do something.'

'All true.'

'Most men would understand where I'm coming from. They would see that it's totally impractical to think about marrying someone you're not in love with for the sake of a child.'

'Also true.'

'But you have to be different, don't you, Leandro?' she said with a mixture of helplessness and frustration. She stood up and walked across to the deep, gleaming stainless steel sink, and stared through the window for a few seconds at a view that couldn't have been more different from the view she had from her kitchen sink, then she turned around, leaned against the counter and stared at him. 'So tell me how this isn't a business deal, and tell me how approaching marriage like a business transaction can *ever* be a good thing.'

'Well,' he said pensively, 'in point of fact, I happen to think that a marriage undertaken as a business proposition stands a far better chance of staying the course. Look at the other options when emotions are involved—either there's the soul-destroying disillusionment once the gold veneer wears off and the rust starts creeping through or, even worse, there's the never-ending high passion that leaves no room for anything else and ends up destroying everything around it.'

'You're so cynical.'

'I'm being realistic, Abby.' Leandro looked at her steadily. 'Set alongside those, a business transaction becomes a gold-plated, blue-chip option. But…' He stood up and strolled towards her and she felt the hairs on the back of her neck stand on end as he drew closer. 'Like I said, this isn't just a business transaction, is it?' He stopped in front of her and leaned forward, caging her in by placing his hands flat on the counter on either side of her.

'Of course it is,' she spluttered.

'Business transactions don't take into account the sort of chemistry we have,' Leandro told her flatly. 'Business transactions are cold, calculated and devoid of the sexual charge that makes it hard for us to keep our hands off one another. In one way, it would make sense for us not to complicate a situation by giving in to what we both want. And of course, if you dig your heels in, then we won't complicate things. We will accept that other people will enter our lives.'

He shrugged. He was playing a wild card, but she could be as stubborn as a mule, and he couldn't appear to force her hand. Under the casual tone of voice and the nonchalant, cool indifference, he found that he was wondering tensely how this would play out. 'I am a highly sexual man,' he admitted. 'I would be unable to remain celibate for any length of time.'

'That's so tacky, Leandro.' But thinking about that made her feel sick.

'I prefer to call it *honest*.' The silence pooled between them and then he leant towards her and feathered his lips over hers. 'And if I'm to be honest again,' he murmured, his voice a caress that made her shiver and that squashed the voice of reason telling her to push him away politely but firmly because this just *wasn't going to do.* 'I would rather be a highly sexual man with you.'

'Leandro…'

'I want you, Abby, and I don't just want you for my wife because you are the mother of my child. I want you for my lover because no other woman has ever turned me on the way you do.'

He kissed her again and this time the kiss was deeper and hungrier. His tongue lashed hers and she moaned softly into his mouth. He took her hand and guided it to the bulge between his legs and he pressed her hand firmly on it. The sensation was exquisite. He was past caring whether he might scare her off. He could feel her *want* radiating from her in waves and it matched his.

Not giving her time to start formulating a bunch of reasons for them to stop, Leandro tugged the prissy white blouse free from her trousers and began unbuttoning it, giving up at some point and tugging it off her, to hell with popping buttons. Pretty soon, she'd have enough money to buy as many prissy white blouses as her heart desired. His big hand curved round her breast possessively and he massaged it through the lacy bra, finding the stiffened bud of her nipple and rolling his thumb over it until her breathing thickened and she was squirming against him.

Wrong, wrong, wrong, her head was yelling, but the truth was that she couldn't get enough of him. She'd *never* been able to get enough of him. She shimmied closer, her hand still feeling his hardness, her whole body keening towards him and resenting the barrier of their clothes.

Still kissing her, Leandro pulled back slightly so that he could get rid of his shirt, then he brushed her hand away, and undid the trousers.

'I'm in heaven,' he breathed hoarsely as her hands curved beneath the opened shirt. He freed her breasts, then unhooked the bra. Without giving her time to think, he swept her off her feet and carried her out of the kitchen and up the flight of stairs to his bedroom. Her feeble protest was met with a plundering kiss that drove all thoughts of resistance straight out of her head.

Her whole body was flushed and trembling as she watched him move quickly towards the shutters, closing them so that the watery afternoon light suddenly became muted. By the time he hit the bed, where he had deposited her, he was unclothed.

Beautiful. He was as beautiful as a statue of a Greek god, all muscle and sinew and a six-pack stomach that was as flat as a washboard. He moved to stand by the bed and she sat up, half-closed her eyes and took him into her mouth.

Leandro breathed in sharply and plunged his fingers into her hair. She knew just how to please him, moving fast then more slowly, her hand gripping him and turning him on in all kinds of places. He only eased her off when he knew that he would climax in her mouth if she carried on, and he wasn't going to do that.

He was going to take her slowly and thoroughly. She wasn't just his lover, she was the mother of his child, and he felt a kick of pride and ferocious possessiveness that he'd never have thought possible.

He undressed her. It was familiar and exciting, rediscovering the body that had always had the ability to drive him out of his mind. When she was naked, he straddled her and looked down at her exquisitely delicate face and her full, beautiful breasts tipped with circular discs that he wanted to lathe with his tongue.

'You drive me wild.' He groaned, and she smiled drowsily at him.

'Less talking.' She reached out and traced the tip of his manhood with her finger, keeping her eyes on his face and loving the reaction that tiny gesture evoked.

Leandro growled a response. 'I was going to take my time…'

'Who said I wanted you to do that?' She wriggled under him and opened her legs, which was his cue to nudge against her. She was so ready for him and he eased his finger into her until she was bucking against his hand. He had to hold himself to contain a driving urge to ejaculate. He couldn't wait. She didn't want him to wait.

He levered himself over her, propped up on both hands and drove into her. She had a body that had always seemed fashioned especially to fit him, sheathing him tightly and taking him to soaring heights of pleasure with the speed of a rocket launching off.

Abigail cried out. Her short, square nails dug into the small of his back and she raised her legs and wrapped them round him as he drove deep and hard into her.

She arched back as she came in an explosion of a thousand fireworks that splintered through her. Her cries were loud and guttural and barely recognisable. With Leandro, she'd learned to lose all her inhibitions. She crested, dimly aware that he, too, was surging towards an orgasm. Wave upon wave of indescribable pleasure rolled over her, an unstoppable tide of sensation that brought tears of real joy to her eyes.

Coming down filled her with such utter contentment that it was hard to remember the gravity of what they had been discussing and the repercussions of decisions that would have to be made. In a gesture born of habit, she sighed and hugged him.

She liked snuggling. Leandro recalled that, just as he recalled that he had enjoyed that too, even though it was something that should have gone against the grain, because he had always been accustomed to vacating the bed pretty much the instant he'd finished having sex with a woman.

Post-coital chit chat had never been his thing, far less cuddles.

On the verge of dozing off, Abigail's eyes flew open and she pulled back and stared at him with horror.

'We didn't use contraception!' She gasped. When he failed to respond with an equal show of horror, she repeated, just in case he'd developed temporary loss of hearing, 'Did you hear what I just said, Leandro? We didn't use any contraception and I'm not on the pill or anything!'

'Marry me, Abigail.' He pulled her back towards him, inserted his thigh between her legs and moved it slowly against her, rousing her all over again.

'Leandro…'

'Can you deny after what we've just done that there isn't a powerful bond between us?'

'Sex isn't a powerful bond,' Abigail denied with a

frightening lack of conviction. 'And is that why you wanted to make love to me? So that you could prove a point? That would be a really hateful thing to do.'

'That's not why I wanted to make love to you,' Leandro said with complete sincerity. 'I wanted to make love to you because I can't resist you.'

'Lust disappears,' she was constrained to point out.

'Most things do but who says that it disappears any faster than all that heady emotion people call *love*? You might be pregnant by me right now.'

'That would be appalling,' Abigail wailed, but he was still doing that thing with his thigh, and she was finding it hard to keep track of why she should be horrified.

She *should* be horrified, shouldn't she? He didn't love her and he never would, and lust *did* fade, and when it did it left nothing behind, nothing concrete that could ever shore up the walls of a relationship. Without love, those fortifications would crumble the minute the sex went off the boil.

But he was still moving his thigh between her legs and she could feel herself climbing again towards a climax. She gyrated against him and orgasmed, shuddering, moaning and clutching his broad shoulders, not caring that he was looking at her flushed face and open mouth, hearing the sounds of her physical satisfaction. In fact, she rather enjoyed the sensation of being observed. It was wanton and really, really sexy.

A thought flew through her head, like quicksilver. *If he didn't mind the thought of getting her pregnant, what did that say?*

It told her one thing and it was that he wanted their relationship to work. He didn't want to marry her with divorce as an option to be kept within sight. If that had been the case, he would never, ever have risked her getting pregnant with a second child.

Could what they had really work? she wondered. In a rush, she saw all the upsides to a situation she had previously discarded as being ridiculous.

Sam would have both parents there for him and that could only be a good thing. When it came to parenthood, you had to put all your selfish traits to one side and do what was best for your child, and she was unwillingly aware that being in a couple with Leandro would be best for their son.

Then there was the little matter of the separate lives he had talked about. If they were together, she wouldn't have to worry about him heading straight into the arms of some woman who wanted to prove that she could be suitable stepmother material. She wouldn't have to face a future riven with jealousy she was forced to conceal.

Because she *would* be jealous. She couldn't bear the thought of him sleeping with anyone else.

Because she was still in love with him.

The realisation didn't jump out at her like a jack-in-the-box, a shocking revelation. It crept out as something she had known all along, deep down. Lust didn't last, but if they both worked truly hard at making things work between them then who was to say that he wouldn't, one day, come to love her the way she loved him? He knew everything there was to know about her now. He knew who she was and where she had come from.

The future suddenly glimmered in front of her, full of possibilities.

'You're not saying anything.' Leandro had a surprising urge for Abigail to put him out of his misery. 'Tell me what you're thinking.'

'I bet that's something you've never asked any woman to do before,' she teased, and he relaxed. It was crazy but he felt quite heady with relief because she wasn't fighting him. He intended to capitalise on that if it killed him.

'Well…?' he pressed impatiently, and Abigail sighed, smiled and looked at the familiar lines of his beautiful face.

'You're right,' she said softly. 'Sam deserves the chance of both parents being there for him. But…' She hesitated and then ploughed on. 'I won't marry you. Let's live together, Leandro. Let's see if we can work together as parents…'

It wasn't what he wanted but he figured that it was a great deal better than nothing. 'If that's how you want to play it,' he conceded gracefully, already making plans to improve on that concession with the greatest possible speed, 'then very well. We'll see if it works between us. For our son's sake.'

CHAPTER SEVEN

ABIGAIL STOOD LOOKING at the little cottage. It was in a beautiful location, forty-five minutes out of London and accessed via picturesque little lanes.

She still had to pinch herself that Leandro was the same man who had pronounced only several weeks ago that the only thing he wanted from her was sex, because as far as he was concerned she was no more than unfinished business waiting for a line to be drawn under it.

When she had decided to tell him about Sam, she hadn't known what to expect. He didn't love her. In fact, he felt the opposite. Nor had marriage ever been on his agenda before. Not even Rosalind, with her impeccable connections and shared social circle, had been able to persuade him otherwise.

Yet, after the initial shock, he had rallied his forces and handled the explosion thrown at him with admirable aplomb. His proposal of marriage had been from a keen sense of duty, which was something she figured out, because the minute he had been given an out he had been happy to accept the far less committed alternative.

Since they had reached the decision to live together nearly two months ago, Leandro had been a model of attentiveness. Anything, it would seem, to further his desire to be a good father. Abigail wasn't entirely surprised, because Leandro always had been a man who threw himself one hundred per cent into everything he did, which was one of the reasons why he had become so successful at such a young age.

Faced with the shock of ready-made fatherhood, he had not run from commitment, but instead had dealt with the situation head on.

It would have been so tempting to think that he had feelings for her and not just for Sam, but she wasn't stupid. He would have married her because, traditionalist to the core, he had seen nothing wrong in making the ultimate sacrifice for the sake of his son. Over the past few weeks, she had come more and more to understand why. Occasionally, when his guard was down, he would let fall little snippets of information about his own childhood and she now had a little more idea of the boy who had become the man.

However, happily released from the duty of putting a wedding ring on her finger, Leandro was doing the next best thing, which was proving to her that he could be the best father possible.

The only fly in the ointment was the fact that she thought that she knew why—once he had proved himself sufficiently, he would walk away from her, safe in the knowledge that she would never try to break the bond he had been at pains to create with Sam. She still felt sick when she thought about him walking away straight into the arms of another woman, but the marriage offer was no longer on the table, and she had had good reasons for turning it down.

Yet everything was so perfect. She just wanted to believe the impossible and she was constantly having to wage war against being lulled into thinking that all the grand gestures meant more than they actually did. But surely, she caught herself thinking more and more as time went on, things were changing between them? To all intents and purposes, they were a couple, and if Leandro didn't have the same feelings for her as she had for him then who was to say that that wouldn't change given time? Hope, she knew, could be as much an enemy as a friend, and she *really* tried to avoid it like the plague, but it still crept in, filling her head with fantasies and presenting a future that was rosy and bright.

This idyllic cottage was definitely high on the 'rosy and bright' spectrum.

'When you said you had a surprise for me, I hadn't expected anything like this,' she murmured, walking towards the chocolate-box white picket fence and then just standing there, lost in pleasant day dreams about how perfect life could be here. She wished they had brought Sam, but at five in the evening it was perilously close to his dinner and bath time, and the nanny Leandro had engaged several weeks previously had persuaded her to leave him back at the apartment. Abigail had been easily swayed, for she knew just how demanding her son could get when he began getting tired and hungry.

'Like it?' Leandro moved smoothly to stand next to her. He couldn't have arranged this on a more pleasant afternoon. Spring was in the air and, although the sun was low, the charm of the place with its climbing roses and neat path to the front door was inescapable.

He had taken great pains to lay it on thick with the estate agent, and it was just the sort of place he was looking for. He could have summed it up thus: *the sort of place I would never normally have glanced at in a million years.*

But, despite her background and the toughness that had seen Abigail through hard times, including the pregnancy she had borne on her own, she was a romantic at heart and that was something he had recognised when they had been seeing each other the first time round. She didn't like his white, modern, minimalist apartment because what she *did* really like was exactly what she was gaping at right now, round-eyed and thrilled to death.

'I absolutely love it.' She turned to him and smiled and, looking down at her, Leandro wanted to do what he *always* seemed to want to do whenever he was anywhere near her—whisk her away like a cave man and have his wicked way with her. She could still get his libido going in five seconds flat and that showed no signs of abating, which was something of a minor miracle, given his predilection towards a fast turn-over when it came to the opposite sex.

'But…' she frowned and looked at him seriously '…we agreed that every decision we took would be one we both wanted, Leandro. Is this sort of place really your kind of thing? It's nothing like your apartment.'

'Should we look inside before we start having this conversation? The place is vacant and the estate agent said we could take our time and then drop the keys back with them through the letter box.'

Abigail looked at the mesmerising beauty of his tanned face and couldn't help falling a little faster

into the seductive hope that all of this thoughtful-
ness might add up to more than just the consider-
ate behaviour of a decent guy who wanted to build
a solid friendship with her before he disappeared
out of her life.

'Okay.' She grinned happily as he unhooked the
gate and ushered her up to the front door. 'I just never
thought that this was your kind of thing...'

'Things are slightly different when there's a child
to consider,' Leandro pointed out and Abigail stifled a sigh because, of course, all of this was being
done for Sam.

After his first uncertain steps in the bonding de-
partment, Leandro had become increasingly confident with his son. From picking him up and holding
him, arms outstretched, with the puzzled expression
of someone not too sure about the wriggling bundle
in his arms, Leandro was now confident enough to
bathe his son, and didn't seem to mind grubby fingers on his expensive clothes. He showed limitless
patience now that Sam was starting to walk and, if
there was one fault, it was that he had a tendency to
overindulge his son with presents that were far too
grown-up for a one-year-old.

'Greyling would have been far too big,' Leandro
pointed out with irrefutable logic, 'and my apartment is, as you've said, far too...*white*. This seemed

a good compromise.' He pushed open the door and in they stepped.

Leandro had visited the place with the estate agent only a couple of days previously. He knew what to expect. Now, he watched as Abigail turned a slow circle in the small hall with its attractive flagstone tiled floor.

'Wow.'

On closer inspection, Leandro could spot a couple of cracked tiles by the wall, but he went along with her enthusiasm as they explored the cottage which was deceptively big and quirkily laid out.

She gushed over everything, from the coving and dado rails, to the range in the kitchen and all the open fireplaces in the rooms. She waxed lyrical about the utility room and the larder. Abigail confessed that never in a million years had she ever thought that she might end up living in a fairy-tale cottage such as this.

They ended up in the garden, which was a riot of flowerbeds and fruit trees.

'Commuting is going to be difficult for you,' Leandro remarked as they sat side by side on a wooden bench placed strategically under one of the apple trees. It was cool but clear and the silence of the countryside felt like an antidote to the chaos and noise of London life.

'I hadn't thought of that,' Abigail responded in some dismay. She had continued with her job, albeit working shorter hours, because she hadn't wanted to lose the small amount of financial independence it afforded her. Deep down she wanted to leave, to spend far more of her time with Sam, but she couldn't bring herself to be so completely dependent on Leandro.

What about when this happy charade ended and Leandro returned to his normal life? Of course, he would ensure that there was a hefty financial settlement involved, but how would she feel about accepting his money and becoming, effectively, a kept woman?

The downside of rejecting his marriage proposal was like the steady drip of acid wearing away all her good intentions, yet what was the point of marriage if it was undertaken for the wrong reasons? The more she was with Leandro, the more she wanted love from him and not duty.

'It wouldn't make sense for you to leave here at a ridiculous hour in the morning to get into London and do a job that you are not required to do in the first place.'

'You don't understand…'

'You're right. I don't understand. You should be overjoyed that there is no financial imperative for you to go out to work.'

Abigail tensed. 'I can't be dependent on you, Leandro. You're being generous because of Sam but, face it, if I hadn't accidentally fallen pregnant then we wouldn't be here now.' She hated the way she hoped that he would refute that, although she couldn't imagine what he could say to do so.

'There's no point dealing in "what if?"s,' Leandro said with deflating logic. 'The fact is that we're at this point now and you have a choice to make. Either you relinquish the job in London and move in here, or we stay at the apartment and you continue working. What's it to be? If you decide that this is the sort of place that would suit you, then say the word and I can have this deal wrapped up by the end of the month.' Leandro turned to her and watched her averted profile like a hawk.

The longer he was with her, the more convinced he was that 'gold-digger' she certainly was not. But he hadn't understood her determination to carry on working, even though the hours had been shortened. Whilst she accepted a modest allowance from him for Sam—far, far less than he would be happy giving her—she still persisted in using her own money to buy anything for herself. He had only just managed to persuade her to stop buying food supplies with what she earned. On the few occasions when he had presented her with items of jewellery, little gifts she could wear out when he took her somewhere flash for dinner, she had accepted, but politely, wearing them once for his benefit then stashing them away in her bedroom drawer.

She got that close but was determined to get no closer and he couldn't blame her. She couldn't forgive him for having walked away from her the first time. She never harked back to it, but why else would she have turned down his marriage proposal? There was still a part of her that distrusted him. Leandro was certain of it.

'I suppose I could work from here…' Abigail flicked a sideways glance at him. He was just so… perfect. If they moved here, would she be letting herself sink ever deeper into a situation from which it would be more and more painful to extract herself? Would this cottage existence with the man of her dreams, the man who didn't love her, just feed the illusion that what they had might end up being the real thing?

Another, darker thought hit her.

Was this his way of removing her from London so that he could gradually resume the life he had put on hold? Was this step one in distancing her from him?

'I expect you'll find it pretty tough to commute from here yourself,' she said lightly, making sure not to look at him, because she didn't want to see her worst suspicions confirmed.

'What are you talking about?'

'Well, it's not exactly next to a railway line, is it?' She forced herself to laugh carelessly. 'If *I* can't commute easily to Central London, then *you* won't be able to either, will you? I mean, you'll have the same problems as I have.'

'I own the company,' Leandro pointed out gently. 'I can work whatever hours I want, and I have a driver to accommodate the travel situation. There isn't the same necessity to get in and leave by certain times. I also don't go to work just to prove a point.'

'I'm not doing that!' Abigail flushed angrily and glared at him.

'Aren't you?' he said wryly and she had the grace to remain silent.

'Anyway, it doesn't matter. I just want you to know that.'

'Sorry, but you've lost me. What doesn't matter?'

'If you need to stay in London overnight.'

'If I need to stay in London *overnight*?'

'Yes. *If* we *both* decide that this is the best place for Sam to grow up, then I don't want you to feel that you have to come home every single evening out of a sense of obligation.'

'It's no obligation when it comes to seeing my son,' Leandro grated, enraged at the not-very-subtle dismissal in her voice.

'I just thought I'd mention it,' Abigail pointed out. 'It's going to be inconvenient for you to be travelling back and forth each day, every day.'

'Why don't you let me decide for myself what I find inconvenient and what I don't?'

She shrugged. 'Sure. Maybe I'll go and have another quick look around before we go.' She sprang to her feet, angry with him for no reason whatsoever.

When he talked about *obligation* it only reinforced her suspicions that the glue that was temporarily binding them together wasn't going to last longer than the blink of an eye. But, whilst being out here would give him ample opportunity gradually to break free, didn't it work both ways? She would gradually get accustomed to having him around less and less. She would be able to distance herself and pull back.

She lost herself in reviewing the cottage all over again and finished up back in the kitchen, and was looking around, when Leandro surprised her from the doorway.

'It'll need work.'

Abigail turned around and looked at him across the width of the kitchen. Due to the lack of furniture, their voices echoed. She hugged herself and raised her eyebrows in a question.

'The cottage,' Leandro said patiently, moving towards her. 'There will be work to be done on it.'

'It's perfect the way it is!' Abigail said immediately, wanting an argument.

'I'm taking it that you have decided that you're happy with the place?'

'I can see myself living here with Sam,' she conceded. 'But I don't want you getting some interior designer in who will get rid of all the traditional features and turn it into a replica of your apartment.'

'Why would I do that?' He strolled towards her and curled his fingers into her silky hair. 'Are you trying to have an argument with me?'

'Of course not. Why would I do that?'

'You *chose* not to change anything in the apartment.'

'I didn't feel comfortable doing that.'

'Your choice. You can do what you like with this place and, for your information, it will be entirely in your name so you don't have to feel that I own the roof over your head.'

'You don't have to do that.' Abigail wondered whether that was another sign of him distancing himself from her.

'I want you to feel secure,' Leandro said gently.

'And I know you're proud, so I don't want you to feel as though you're indebted to me. You're the mother of my child and I intend to look after you.'

He tilted her chin and feathered a kiss on her mouth, at which point her defence system was well and truly knocked for six. Of their own accord, her arms lifted, curved around his neck and pulled him towards her.

Sex. It always came back to this. Aside from his sense of duty, it was the thing that powered their relationship but, oh, how it left her feeling vulnerable. Yet, she couldn't help but take what was on offer, torn between making the most of what she had while she had it and trying to resist so that she could start building her defences for when they parted company.

And there were times, such as now, when he was just so *nice* that she didn't have it in her to resist him.

He could be so tough, so ridiculously forceful, yet at other times so unbearably tender that it took her breath away and left her feeling as helpless as a kitten.

She kissed him back, holding his face in her hands, and whispered guiltily, 'We *can't*.'

'But I'm hungry for you, Abigail. Ravenous.'

'Is sex the only thing you think about?' she half-joked.

'Is it my fault that you continue to do crazy things to my libido?' He drew back and smoothed her hair with slightly less steady hands than he would have liked.

She was wearing a pair of jeans and a long-sleeved red tee shirt under a trench coat and she looked amazing. Fresh, wholesome, shockingly pretty and absolutely lacking in artifice.

'I admit it wouldn't be right to make love here,' he conceded with obvious reluctance. 'What sex on the ground gains in reckless impulse, it loses in sheer discomfort.' He grabbed her hand and headed out of the cottage, carefully locking the door behind them and putting paid to any impulse she might have had to do another quick turn round the place.

He reversed at a pace back into the road. 'But I can't wait until we get back to London.'

'Don't be outrageous, Leandro.'

'You make me outrageous.' He shot her a look that was bone-meltingly sincere, and Abigail shivered and wondered whether he knew just how achingly addictive he could be without even realising it.

Soon he was gunning along the lanes, dusk falling steadily around them. With no traffic to speak of, they would have been back in London in less than two hours, so she was surprised when he swung the snazzy silver sports car into the courtyard of a country pub that was as picture-postcard perfect as the cottage had been.

'I said I couldn't wait,' he growled.

Not even stopping to enjoy a glass of wine, they headed for the room he had rented for the sake of an hour and made love, wild, passionate love, that left her weak and clinging to him and crazily, stupidly happy.

'That was such a decadent use of money,' she giggled as they headed back down to London. 'And what must that poor hotel manager be thinking?'

'That he got a good deal,' Leandro remarked wryly. 'He rented us his most expensive suite and we were there for under an hour. He's laughing all the way to the bank. Tomorrow I'm going to seal the deal with the house.' He reached out and covered her hand with his. 'Will you leave the job, Abby?'

Was that why he had made that very unusual detour? she wondered with unexpected cynicism. He knew that she was putty in his hands when they made love. But, no, she couldn't credit him with that amount of deviousness, even though he *was* a man who was accustomed to getting what he wanted at whatever the cost.

'I guess I will,' she said at last, knowing that she truly did want to spend her time with Sam, even if it meant giving Leandro his way. 'But I shall miss working there. Vanessa has been very good to me and I owe her a huge debt of gratitude.'

'So do I,' Leandro said gravely and she looked at him in surprise.

'What do you mean?'

'I mean,' he glanced at her briefly, 'It's bad enough thinking of you broke and down on your luck while you were pregnant, but it's worse when I think of what might have happened if you hadn't had that lifeline extended to you.'

Sam was asleep by the time they returned to Leandro's apartment at a little after seven-thirty. The nanny—a lovely young woman who absolutely adored the baby—spent a few minutes telling them what escapades he had got up to in their absence, and as soon as she had gone they both went into the room which had been turned into his nursery and gazed down at their son.

Typically, no expense had been spared in the decoration of the room. The walls were a pale blue with a hand-painted scene from a popular children's movie on one of the walls. In the corner of the room, a tepee had been erected with a sheepskin rug in which he could cocoon himself. Next to the tepee was a giant stuffed toy—a surprise present from Leandro, bought a couple of weeks previously.

Leandro gazed down at Sam and Abigail gazed furtively at Leandro. The only light in the room came from a tiny night light. Her heart clenched, for this was what it looked like to see him shorn of his toughness. His face was softened in the mellow glow. He had never looked at her like that, with open tenderness, and once upon a time she might have thought that he was incapable of that depth of emotion. He wasn't. She squeezed his arm and he glanced across at her.

She padded down to the kitchen, where food had been prepared for them by the housekeeper who came in daily to make sure that the apartment always resembled something you would see in a fancy interior-design magazine.

For some reason, the thought of leaving London made her feel all shaken up. She had burrowed into a comfort zone here, in this apartment, with one foot still connected to her old life working at the jewellery store and another placed squarely here, surrounded by this unbelievable luxury.

But now everything was changing and that unsettled her. The future seemed shakier than ever and she realised that, without even being aware of it, she had rooted herself into the pretence of thinking that what they had was a real relationship instead of a stitched-together one for the sake of their child. She had subconsciously latched on to the changes she had seen in Leandro—his attentiveness, his consideration, his real efforts at being a dad—and had translated them into something they weren't.

Not once had he ever expressed any feelings towards her. He knew how to make her feel sexy, and he was eloquent on the subject of her physical attributes and what effect they had on him, but that was where it all ended.

Now, she would be moving out of London, giving up her job, and whatever Leandro said now about being able to handle the commute she knew that it wouldn't be long before he settled into a pattern of overnighting at the apartment when he had to work late. And how long before he was tempted to relax in his apartment with a woman to massage away the stress of the day?

Of course, he would still see Sam, but it wouldn't be long before he would suggest having Sam on his own, and by then Sam would be old enough to stay overnight with him.

Abigail knew that she should be taking one day at a time instead of projecting down the road but, as she began dealing with the food that had been prepared, she could feel a thousand possible scenarios zipping in and out of her mind like angry, buzzing wasps.

She surfaced to find Leandro lounging in the

doorway, arms folded, his amazing eyes fastened to her face.

'Spit it out,' he said without preamble. 'What's going on?'

'Nothing!'

'Then why are you looking as though you've suddenly realised that the sky might start falling down?'

He strolled towards her but before she could scrabble to provide a reason for her sudden, unexpected shift of mood his mobile phone buzzed in his pocket and he held up one hand to silence her.

Standing only inches away from him, Abigail heard a woman's voice and all the fears which had been playing out in her head congealed into the certainty that this was why Leandro was suddenly so keen to shift her out of London to the house of her dreams.

Not only was he talking to a woman, but he had lowered his voice and was leaving the kitchen.

He was on the phone to a woman and he didn't want her to overhear the conversation.

Gripped with a sickening sense of apprehension, she remained glued to the spot until he reappeared in under five minutes, shoving the phone back into his pocket as he strode back into the kitchen. He should have been looking as guilty as the worst of sinners but there wasn't a trace of guilt etched on those devastating features.

Abigail kicked herself for even thinking that she should expect him to feel guilty because he had been talking to a woman on the phone, having an intimate conversation he hadn't wanted her to overhear. But *still*...

'Who was that?' she was horrified to hear herself ask, in an accusatory voice, and Leandro stilled and looked at her with veiled eyes.

Every instinct in him rallied and railed against the querulous note in her voice. 'No one that should concern you,' he offered coolly.

Trembling, because as fast as that he had become a stranger just because she had asked him something he hadn't wanted to hear, Abigail dug her heels in and stood her ground.

'You were talking to a woman,' she flung at him.

'I do not want to get into this, Abigail.'

'But you were, weren't you?'

'Would you say that that's a crime?' Leandro asked tautly. Unaccustomed to having to justify his behaviour, he had reverted to type. Did he want to argue with her? No. 'You need to calm down and not over-excite yourself about it.'

'Who was she?' Abigail demanded. 'No!' She held up an imperious hand, shaking like an engine at full throttle. 'Don't bother telling me. You don't have to. You can do exactly as you please. I don't care!'

'Don't you?' he asked with considerable intent, eyes narrowed on her flushed face.

'Of course I don't!' She spun away to gather herself, took a few deep breaths and then looked at him with a lot more control than she felt. 'I apologise for having questioned you,' she offered. 'We don't owe one another anything and I realise that.'

'Even though we're lovers?' Leandro questioned and she waved that aside.

'We both know that that doesn't mean anything.' She cleared her throat. 'You can do as you please.'

'So you wouldn't mind if that woman on the phone was someone I intended to sleep with?'

Pain slithered through her as sharp as broken glass. 'Of course, I would expect you to break off our relationship before you start hopping into bed with someone else.'

'I don't believe I'm hearing this,' Leandro muttered darkly.

Abigail ignored him. In fact, she barely heard what he'd said. She was far too taken up with the images racing through her head, like a cinematic reel on fast-forward.

'How long will it take before I can move into the cottage with Sam?' she asked, already settling on that as the only way to break the catastrophic effect he had on her. If he wanted to carry on with some other woman, then she wasn't going to be around to witness it in the shape of late arrivals back and un-avoidable meetings.

It was astounding that he could seem so preoc-cupied with her, so crazily *in lust* with her, and still make time to start playing the field. Just thinking about it ripped her to shreds and she could feel tears beginning to glaze the back of her eyes.

'Well?' she demanded forcefully and his lips thinned.

'I will sort out the finances tomorrow and I can have the whole place brought up to scratch in record time. You can be in within the fortnight.'

CHAPTER EIGHT

LEANDRO STARED OUT of his office window, brow pleated in a frown of dissatisfaction.

He couldn't concentrate and he loathed that. He had cancelled three meetings in the past ten days and had rescheduled his trip to New York for the following month. Right at this moment, his secretary was under strict instructions to hold all outside calls, even though the documents he should be getting through while all those calls were being conveniently held were still sitting in front of him on his computer, waiting to be checked.

Scowling, he vaulted upright and strolled towards the window to gaze down at an unseasonably fine spring afternoon.

Everything was coming along a pace. The cottage had been bought and without a chain, or the thorny problem most people faced of having to get a mortgage, he had been able to rush things along and work had already started on some essential renovations.

He had discussed those renovations with Abigail in the atmosphere of cool politeness that had characterised the time they now spent together.

She'd made a fuss over that phone call and had assumed the worst of him and when he had, quite rightly, put his foot down at launching into a grovelling explanation of a simple phone call, she had resorted to the oldest female trick in the book. The cold shoulder.

And no sex.

God only knew exactly what was going through her head but it didn't take the IQ of a genius to figure out that whatever outlandish scenario she was conjuring up probably involved him in a compromising position with a woman.

Frustrated beyond measure, he cursed softly under his breath.

This entire episode could have been avoided, he knew, if he had simply told her that he had been speaking to his sister, but the conversation with Cecilia had been an unusually abrupt and inconclusive one and he had been in no mood to deal with Abigail's crazy suspicions.

Why should he?

He'd never had much time for people who made demands of him. What man did? A demanding woman always turned possessive at some point and there was no way he would ever contemplate having any such relationship.

It infuriated him that, after all those very reasonable pep talks he had given himself in the past week and a half, he was still out of sorts. He hated the saccharine smile she produced every time he walked through the front door and, for the past few days, she had somehow managed either to ensure that the nanny had dinner with them or had invited Vanessa or one of the other employees of the shop over so that any time spent alone together had been frankly reduced to zilch.

And then there was the lack of sex.

Leandro couldn't work out how it was that he missed her warm, willing and incredibly sexy body so much.

Sex was a bodily function, wasn't it? A very pleasant bodily function but nothing upon which the entire world could stop turning on its axis if it wasn't around.

And yet...

He glanced at his watch, noting the slow passage of time and cursing the tendency to introspection that seemed suddenly and inexplicably to have taken up residence in him.

It took a lot of focus and concentration actually to get down to reviewing the complicated legalese that had to be picked over for the deal he was in the process of closing and, the next time he looked at his watch, it was after seven.

For the first time since she had re-entered his life as the mother of his child, Abigail was going out for the evening. She had handed in her notice and Vanessa was throwing her a little party at a club not a million miles away. Not only were the employees of the company invited, along with a few of Abigail's friends she had made during the time she had been working in London, but some of their more regular clients who had dealt with her over the years were also going to be there.

This information had not been volunteered by Abigail, but by Vanessa, when she had come over two evenings previously for dinner. Leandro had surreptitiously scrutinised Abigail's face for a show of excitement but he hadn't been able to glean a thing from her lack of expression.

But he had had to face the stark truth, which was that they were no longer sleeping together and, effectively, she was a single woman who could do as she liked.

Which, of course, would be nothing, because if there was one thing he had worked out it was that she wasn't the sort to jump into bed with a man just because the opportunity happened to present itself.

He almost laughed at the thought of her going to some office party and throwing herself around.

Yes, they would be going to a club, and indeed he knew the club they would be going to and had once been a regular there back in the day. And yes, sure, there would be music and dancing, although he personally had never been one of those gyrating on a dance floor, but doubtless she would miss Sam and would make her excuses to leave as early as possible.

He'd bet on it.

Abigail looked at her reflection in the mirror of the spare room she now occupied. The wardrobe spanned one entire wall and was completely mirrored. There was no escaping the reflection staring back at her. It felt odd to be dressed up when she had spent so many months in an array of unexciting work garb or old stay-at-home clothes that were suitable for holding a baby.

Since Leandro had re-entered her life, her wardrobe had undergone a radical transformation because he had insisted that she buy herself stuff she could go out in. He had even bought a couple of dresses for her himself, which had seemed extraordinary at the time, but she had quietly put those to the back of the wardrobe because she was assailed by a weird feeling of guilt whenever she thought about wearing them.

She'd extracted one of those dresses now and she had to admit that it fit like a dream.

It was figure-hugging, short and, despite the very modest neckline and three-quarter-length sleeves, still managed to look incredibly sexy.

Maybe because it was fire-engine red. For better or for worse, one look at her and people would stop dead in their tracks, and that was exactly what she wanted them to do because her confidence levels were at an all-time low.

Things between Leandro and herself had changed so quickly from wonderful to nightmarish.

One phone call.

Why couldn't he have told her what it had been about? How hard would it have been for him just to have said that he had been on the phone to a work colleague? Very hard, she reckoned, if that phone call had been from a prospective lover, and surely it had been or he would have explained the situation?

He was seeing someone else. Or, at the very least, he was contemplating it.

Abigail couldn't bear the thought of it. When she had heard a woman's voice down the end of the line, the jealousy that had gripped her had been as powerful as a vice squeezing her heart. Since then she had feverishly found herself imagining *what* woman. Blonde? Brunette? Tall? Short? Past flame? Potential flame? She'd been driven crazy with her imagining.

And, when she hadn't been busy *imagining,* she had been sensible enough to work out that their trial period—which she could now see she had optimistically undertaken in the wild hope that he would find himself loving her, and proposing to her all over again for the right reasons—was at an end.

She had taken herself off to the spare room on the night of the phone call. Leandro hadn't objected. He had watched her move her stuff out and close the door on sex and he hadn't tried to win her back. Considering the sex had been so powerful, that pretty much said it all as far as she was concerned.

Her heart was breaking, but she was keeping it together, trying to make sure that she behaved like an adult for Sam's sake. She wasn't going to run away or take out her sadness and hurt by being mean to Leandro. Once upon a time, she'd let her emotions determine her behaviour and had deprived him of the first ten months of his son's life and, looking back, she could see that although she had done that without malevolence she'd been misguided.

So she was polite to him. They made conversation. She kept her distance and communicated the way she would have communicated with a perfect stranger, even though every time she looked at his lean, achingly beautiful face her heart squeezed tighter and the hollow in the pit of her stomach hurt more.

She would have to move on with her life, whilst recognising that he would still be a part of it whether she liked it or not. She would still have to see him. When she moved out to the cottage, he would probably show up one day with the very woman he had been talking to on the phone in that guilty, hushed voice. And she would have to face her replacement with equanimity and get on with it.

'Getting on with it' meant having a life of her own. She'd decided that step one to achieving that would be to go out to the party Vanessa had arranged and have fun.

Hence the dress. And the make-up, which was deceptively light but definitely effective. And the hair, which she'd had styled at the hairdressers. Trimmed and straightened, it hung down to her waist in a colourful golden curtain.

She had already settled Sam and, sticking her feet into some very high sandals, she had a few quick words with the nanny and then hurried out to get into the taxi which she had ordered earlier. She could easily have taken Leandro's driver, but not relying on such luxuries seemed a vital step in reasserting the independence which she had gradually forfeited during the time she had spent succumbing to Leandro's charms and nurturing hopeless fantasies about happy-ever-afters.

The club was in the centre of London and by

the time Abigail got there, having texted Vanessa to warn her that she would be arriving—so that she didn't turn up at the place and find herself on her own, having to order a drink at a bar and hope she didn't look as if she had been stood up by a hot date—it was already heaving.

Taking a deep breath, she headed in, very much aware of heads swinging in her direction, and decided that she was going to have fun if it killed her.

Leandro wasn't quite sure how, at a little after nine-thirty, he found himself outside the club where Abigail's leaving party was taking place. It seemed that one minute he'd been engrossed in the finer points of due diligence, and the next he'd been in the back of his car on his way to Valentino's.

Outside, there was a polite gathering of well-heeled, well-dressed thirty-somethings, mostly smoking and holding flutes of champagne. The men had dispensed with their obligatory jackets but the women were still decked out in their finery, even if they were beginning to look a little less groomed than they had probably looked two hours previously.

The doormen looked bored. Valentino's was an exclusive members-only club and the opportunities for getting rid of riff raff would be remote.

Leandro wasn't sure where his membership card was, but in any event it didn't matter because he was known here. He also carried that air of unassailable power and opulence that encouraged people to bow, scrape and open doors before they even realised what doors they were opening.

It had been well over a year since he had been there, but he was familiar with the layout. Like other private clubs, this was a dark, intimate place, with a very cleverly thought out décor that encouraged intimacy, relaxation and therefore a great deal of expensive drinking and eating. The bar snacks were unusually good and the food, which was served in separate rooms, had won Michelin stars. To one side, the actual bar was a curving oak semi-circle that brought to mind old-fashioned movies involving the mafia. The dance floor was a raised podium with low lighting and sufficient space to house a live band, which was often the case, although not tonight. Sofas and comfortable chairs were interspersed between low wooden tables.

As always, the place was heaving. Jean Claude, a Frenchman of impeccable good manners and frightening efficiency, ran the show with a hand of steel. Drinks were never spilled, bar snacks were always delivered with aplomb, food was never served cold.

Leandro had been prepared to cut short the preliminaries and flatly ask him where Abigail's party could be found, but he didn't have to because, eyes narrowed, he saw for himself where his quarry was.

He clenched his jaw and remained standing where he was, towards the back of the dark room, a towering, vaguely menacing presence that was attracting all sorts of sidelong looks from the people edging past him.

No wonder Abigail hadn't waxed lyrical about the leaving party, he thought through gritted teeth. She had managed very successfully to keep her excitement under wraps.

She'd barely had time for him for the past couple of weeks. Indeed, they had moved seamlessly from passionate lovers to nodding acquaintances—but what a fool he would have been to have thought that she might have been missing…well, missing *him*.

It appeared not.

It seemed that she had been ticking off the days until she could let her hair down and revert to the single life she had clearly never intended to leave behind.

So much for that sweet, sexy smile and those big doe eyes when she had told him that she wouldn't marry him, but would live with him and see how things went. She'd failed to mention that the slightest hiccup and she'd be off in a puff of smoke.

Every muscle tensed, he watched through narrowed eyes as she danced with some guy who looked as though he would have jumped all over her given half a chance. Her eyes were half-closed and her movements were as rhythmic as a professional dancer's. Around her, everyone else faded in comparison. It was as if she exuded an unbearably bright glow which was, quite literally, unmatchable.

The over-eager man curved his hand around her waist to gather her closer and Leandro didn't wait to see how she would react.

Galvanised into furious action, he strode through the crowds, the tables and the waitresses holding huge, circular trays above their heads. By the time he hit the dance floor, fury was coursing through every vein in his body. He made no effort to think straight or to analyse why he was behaving the way he was.

'Mind if I cut in?' He barely glanced at the younger man who stepped back with an expression of alarm. Every scrap of his attention was reserved for the woman who had now snapped to attention and was frowning at him in a way that suggested perhaps one glass of champagne too many.

'How much have you had to drink?' he demanded.

Abigail blinked and laboriously tried to work out an answer to that, while trying to process the unexpected appearance of Leandro in the middle of the dance floor. He'd appeared out of nowhere—and he wasn't dancing.

The music had changed from upbeat to a ballad and she tugged the lapels of his white shirt and shimmied closer to him. 'Can I interest you in a dance?'

Aware that the eyes of the world were beadily swivelling in their direction, Leandro curved his big body against hers, shifting and settling her against him so that he could murmur into her ear, 'I'm dancing. Now, how much have you had to drink? No, scratch that. Who the hell was that guy you were dancing with? If I hadn't arrived in time, you would have had to peel him off you…or was that what you wanted? Have I interrupted a romance in the making?'

He tightened his grip on her and pulled her a little closer. Her breasts were pushing against him. When he thought of that guy and pictured him getting into a clinch like this with her, Leandro saw red, and he had to bite down the urge to find the man and thrash the living daylights out of him.

It would never happen, of course. Leandro abhorred that sort of extreme reaction. And yet…*his fingers itched…*

'I haven't had *much* to drink.' Abigail knew that her inhibitions were lowered. She had come to have a good time and had knocked back three glasses of champagne in quick succession in her quest not to be a party pooper.

The champagne had gone to her head, and had done wonderful things to loosen her up and relieve her of some of the terrible stress and sadness that had been plaguing her every day since she and Leandro had begun pulling away from one another.

Right now, it was also allowing her really to enjoy the firmness of his body against hers and the husky, urgent whisper in her ear and that tone of...*possessiveness* was frankly thrilling.

She cosied up to him and he didn't pull away.

'Shane,' she murmured, curving her hands behind his neck and linking her fingers together.

'Shane?' The woman was sex on legs and Leandro's blood ran more hot the closer she pressed herself against him. He fought to remember that this was the same demanding woman who had laid into him simply because he had failed to answer a question which should never have been asked in the first place. He didn't do nagging, even though she was in a different category from anyone else who'd ever tried. However, his body was not making the necessary connections, and he knew if he wasn't careful soon he'd be as hard as steel and painfully in need of relief.

'Don Andrew's son.' Abigail was proud of her ability to think clearly even though she knew that the drink had gone to her head. 'Don Andrew,' she enunciated with precision and clarity, 'is a regular customer of ours. Shane is his son by his first marriage. He came in with his girlfriend a couple of months ago to buy a diamond bracelet for her.'

'And where's the lucky girl now?' Leandro bit out. 'Hiding behind a pillar? Waiting for him to get back to her just as soon as he's done making a pass at you?'

Abigail pulled back and stared at him in apparent fascination. 'Are you *jealous*?'

Leandro flushed darkly. 'I don't do jealousy,' he denied, voice cool and clipped. 'Never have, never will. You've had too much to drink. I'm taking you home.'

'But I've only just got here,' Abigail trilled. 'And we've barely danced together at all.' She pouted up at him, all lush pink lips and bedroom eyes, and Leandro swore softly and fluently under his breath.

'Don't do that,' he said roughly. They'd managed to find their way to the side of the dance floor where the light was even dimmer and the music was low enough that they could hear themselves talk.

'Do what?' She fluttered her lashes with a shameful lack of reserve and giggled.

'Ask for something you might not be intending to ask for,' Leandro growled. Never had self-restraint felt so hard, and his desire was so painful he could barely move properly.

'Maybe I am intending to ask for what you don't think I should be *intending* to ask for…or something like that…' She pulled him down towards her because she just had to, and her body went up in flames as his cool lips met hers, then lingered and then devoured, tongues meshing, her little moans shattering proof of how much she'd missed touching him.

Leandro was the first to pull back and he was shaking as he raked his fingers through his hair. 'I don't believe in these public displays of affection.' He looked at her long and hard, and wanted her with every bone and muscle and tendon in his big body. 'Besides, you're not in control. Where's your boss? I'm taking you to her, and you're going to make your excuses and then we're going home. And don't even think of telling me that you're *not ready to go yet.*'

Leandro didn't give Abigail time to mull anything over. They were out of the club in under ten minutes and in his car, heading back to the apartment. She was pressed against him, her body soft and pliable like a rag doll, and it took the will power of a saint to keep his hands to himself.

He would settle her into the spare room and in the morning she would wake up with a thumping headache and there would be no question of him having taken advantage of her.

That plan worked pretty much until he'd shut his bedroom door. He'd settled her into her room, having made sure to check on Sam. He'd even made sure she'd wriggled out of the cling-film dress which, if he had his way, no other man would get to see her in again. He'd politely turned his back, in true *ex*-lover style, while she'd got into whatever sleeping clothes she'd found in one of the drawers after she'd banged about searching. Then he'd reminded her that there were paracetamol in the cabinet in her *en suite* bathroom, and told her to take two, because she wouldn't like how she'd feel when she woke up in the middle of the night.

Then he'd gritted his teeth in pure frustration and taken to his bedroom and then…

And then his door had opened and she'd been there.

As quiet as a wraith and as beautiful as the most tempting of sirens.

And, as she'd climbed onto the bed with him, Leandro reckoned that he was, after all, just flesh and blood.

Now, as she lay staring intently at him in the silvery light filtering through the shutters, he sighed and shook his head.

'I want this,' Abigail said, as sober as a judge. She could scarcely credit that she had walked into his bedroom, which was next to hers, as naked as the day she'd been born, not caring about the consequences. She wanted him and she was sick to death of telling herself that wanting him was no way to move on with her life. Being a martyr hurt like hell, especially when they were both living under the same roof. For one night, she didn't want to be a martyr. Having lost him, she had woken up to how much she had lost, and it hurt more than she could ever have thought.

'I'm not going to take advantage of you.'

'No, you're not,' Abigail agreed. '*I'm* going to take advantage of *you*.'

He laughed in exasperation as Abigail unbuttoned his trousers and pulled them off before working on his shirt. He was the very picture of a man who was exercising as much self-restraint as he possibly could and she loved him—yes, loved him—for that.

Loved him even though he didn't love her and even though he probably had some stupid woman in the background ready to take her place. Abigail loved him so much that she wanted to take what was here right now and think about the consequences later. After all, she'd have a lifetime to pay her dues, wouldn't she?

She pushed him onto his back and climbed onto him, moving slowly and sinuously against his bare chest while she eased the shirt over his shoulders, only pausing and shifting so that he could rid himself of it. Leandro seemed to give in to his desire and put up no resistance.

'Don't let me get in the way of you taking advantage of me,' he said huskily with a smile that turned her on even more, from the soles of her feet to the top of her head. He hooked his thumb provocatively under the waistband of his boxers and tugged it suggestively, just enough to show her how aroused he was, then smiling the smile of the victor when her eyelids fluttered and she moaned softly.

'Have your wicked way with me, my darling, because I've missed you.'

Don't say stuff like that, she wanted to yell, because lines like that were what had got her where she was now, had made her think that there was more to what they had than there actually was.

When he said that he *missed* her, what he really meant was that he'd *missed the sex.*

Which meant that there wasn't another woman. Not yet. Because he wouldn't be here if there was. She just knew that.

Right now, she just wanted to hold him tight. She planted her hands on either side of him and leant over, lowering her breasts for him to take into his mouth, a nipple at a time. Head flung back, she groaned without restraint as he laved one hardened nipple with his tongue, while holding her other breast and massaging it. He moved between the two and took his time.

Then he cupped her behind and Abigail daringly edged up, straddling him and inching her way towards his mouth in small, sinuous stages until she positioned herself just where his tongue could flick devastatingly against her. He tickled her with the tip of his tongue and she released a long, shuddering moan. Her breathing was shallow and fast and, as he continued to taste her between her legs, she moved against his mouth. She felt little shivers of excitement racing like quicksilver through her veins, signalling an orgasm if she didn't stop to gather herself, but for a little while longer she enjoyed what his mouth was doing.

He was big and hard for her when it was her turn to taste him. Leandro angled her body, sliding her over him, and they tasted one another.

He couldn't get enough of her. He'd gone mad when he'd seen her dancing on that dance floor, seen the way other men had been eyeing her, and the way that guy had been circling her, waiting to make his move.

Was it simply possessiveness?

Something weird and disconcerting kicked inside him and he buried the odd sensation in the only way he knew how.

With sex.

He took over and Abigail loved it. He was so powerful and yet tender between the sheets. Her body was thrumming when, after an eternity, he thrust into her with long, deep strokes that drove her wild. Fingers biting into his waist, she moved against him, finding the rhythm that was theirs and moving to its beat, their bodies as one as sensation built and built between them.

She climaxed on a wave of shuddering ecstasy that went on and on and on, taking her to ever higher peaks which were made all the more amazing because she knew that he was coming as well, his body arching and stiffening under the impact of his own orgasm.

In sex, they truly became one person.

As they descended back down to Planet Earth, Abigail marvelled that she could have translated that complete physical union as a uniting of the mind, soul and spirit as well.

And what, she wondered in sudden raw confusion, was she going to do now?

He was back in bed with her and she didn't want to let him go, but thinking like that made her feel like a coward after the stand she had taken. How could she love someone who was so indifferent to her that he'd point-blank refused to answer a simple question? When he knew that the answer would have meant so much to her? They might not be married, but they'd been lovers and parents to a child. How did secrecy fit into that scenario?

Bitter tears tried to push their way through as stark regret began to invade her. Yet when Leandro scooped her against him she was happy to let him. She flattened her hands against his chest and breathed him in deeply, then sighed.

'Okay,' Leandro told her roughly. 'You win.'

Abigail drew back and squirmed into a position that allowed her look at him. 'What have I won?'

'You asked me who I was talking to on the phone.'

'You don't have to tell me anything you don't want to,' she lied with a dull flush. 'And it's not some kind of game, Leandro. We were supposed to be... *trying*...and it...it *hurt* thinking that you were talking to a woman on the phone. And it *hurt* to realise that you couldn't even respect what we had enough to tell me who it was. I know I have no rights over you but you wanted to know who that guy was... the one I was dancing with...and I told you. You'd rather walk away than tell me and, for me, that could only mean you were talking to someone you plan on sleeping with.'

Leandro groaned, lay flat on his back and stared up at the ceiling because everything she said made sense. He'd been an idiot and he couldn't blame her for laying into him. He'd let his pride rule him. 'I'm not accustomed to...answering to other people,' he admitted gruffly. 'But I should have just told you and I... I apologise.'

Abigail closed her eyes for a few seconds, astounded that she had won this concession, and astounded that he had apologised to her. True, it wasn't a flowers-and-chocolates kind of apology, but she knew instinctively how much it took for someone like Leandro to say sorry, someone who didn't, as he had said, *answer to other people.*

'So, who was it?' she asked coolly, pressing him for an answer.

'My sister. I was talking to Cecilia.'

CHAPTER NINE

ABIGAIL STIFFENED AND drew away from him. Aside from that one conversation two months ago, Cecilia had not been mentioned. Where was she? She could have set up residence on Mars, for all Abigail knew. Leandro never mentioned her, and Abigail knew better than to initiate any conversation about her, because she was all too aware of the unshakeable bond between them. At least, out of their sight, she could do no more damage—although why on earth hadn't Leandro said at the time who he had been talking to? Unless the conversation had been an awkward one. And it didn't take a genius to figure out what that *awkward* subject might have been.

'How is she?' Abigail asked, trying to sound concerned, and Leandro looked at her wryly.

'I'm sensing real interest there,' he remarked, but his face was serious and thoughtful and she couldn't help but feel a wave of unease. He would always at least partly believe the picture Cecilia painted of herself and presented to him. Lately, it might have taken a dent, and perhaps he wasn't quite as forgiving in his responses as once he might have been, but essentially Cecilia could do no wrong. She was his kid sister, he had always taken care of her, and caretaking was a habit that could never be broken.

'She hasn't been around.' Abigail lay flat on her back, pulled the duvet up to cover her nakedness and stared at the ceiling, although in her mind's eye she could see his face, shuttered and inward thinking.

'That's because she's been on the other side of the world opening up my boutique hotel in Fiji. It's been non-stop for her. She's barely had time to surface. She's also got involved with one of the project managers working with her, so she hasn't had any interest in flying back to the UK when she can holiday on a South Pacific island if she needs a break.'

'Why didn't you tell me that she was the woman you were talking to on the phone?' Abigail demanded, turning to look at his profile.

'Like I said,' Leandro returned without missing a beat, 'I'm not accustomed to having questions asked about who I'm talking to, or where I'm going or with whom.'

Abigail inhaled deeply. 'I know we're not married,' she began, 'and that in fact you'd probably feel the same way even if we *were* married, but as far as I'm concerned that's not an acceptable attitude to take.'

'Come again?' Leandro turned to her, astounded that she would flatly choose to start an argument when he had earlier offered her an apology for not having told her what she had wanted to know, and when he had volunteered the information in a move that, for him, was a massive concession.

Abigail wasn't going to back down on this but the brooding disapproval in those eyes was wreaking havoc with her levels of courage. 'I mean you need to make a choice, and then we can take things from there.'

'I'm not following you,' he replied, but all his senses were on red alert. He shifted so that he was on his side and they were looking at one another, eye to eye. It hadn't escaped him that she had tugged the covers up to cover herself, and from that he gathered that this was a serious conversation, a conversation in which accidental nudity had no part. 'What choice am I supposed to be making?'

'We're living together,' Abigail began with a great deal more assuredness than she was feeling. Indeed, she was floundering so much inside that she marvelled that her voice hadn't dried up completely. 'You may think that I overreacted to your silence, but I've had real doubts as to whether it's a good idea to let something develop between us.' She sighed and looked at his shuttered, unrevealing face. At least he hadn't turned away. At least he was listening. As far as she was concerned that was a case of so far, so good.

'Did you honestly think that I was on the phone to another woman? Planning a *rendezvous* with her—whilst sleeping with you? On the one hand, I'm flattered that you think my energy levels are through the roof, but on the other hand I'm insulted that you would even think that I might be capable of what you have accused me of.'

'I haven't accused you of anything but there's no room for those sorts of silences between us. If you really feel that there's no need for you to ever explain your actions, or tell me where you've been if I ask, then say so right now and I will pack my bags and leave this apartment in the morning. I'll move into the cottage with Sam, and I will never, ever try and limit your contact with him, but there will never be anything more between us. You'll be free to do whatever you like, without anyone questioning you. In essence, you would be free to remain a bachelor and behave like one—but if we're to be together then, as far as I'm concerned, you might not be married but you're no longer a bachelor.'

Just like that, Leandro knew that the rules of the

game had changed and, whilst instinct was telling him to make a stand—a *justified* stand, because the only rules he had ever played to had been his own—there was a third party involved.

Was he prepared to risk his relationship with his son? Because, say what she might at this point in time, if he chose to turn his back on her now, when she had effectively told him that she was prepared to give it another go, his rejection would fester inside her, and everyone knew that old saying about a woman scorned.

And the world was full of men ready and willing to try it on with her, even if she came with a child. She had the sort of looks that guaranteed that she wouldn't be left on the shelf for longer than five seconds. Everything in him demanded Abigail remain *his*.

'If you insist on terms and conditions,' Leandro drawled, 'then I have a couple of my own.'

'You still haven't answered what I asked.'

'I will do my utmost…' he flushed darkly and she met his accompanying glare with serenity '…to keep you in the loop and, if you're curious about any of my activities—which I assure you will be above board, whatever you might think—then I will satisfy your curiosity with the appropriate explanations.'

'Okay.' She paused and registered the heady relief flooding her because the past days had been hellish and she knew, seeing him tonight, that she just wanted him back whether it made sense or not. 'What are your terms and conditions?'

'You don't turn your back on me and play the *no sex* card every time you want to make a point. I understand that you were hurt, but don't think you can try to turn me into a person I will never be and then, if you think your efforts are failing, decide to withdraw sex.'

A person who will never be in love with me, Abigail thought bravely, *because if you were in love with me, compromising would come as second nature. It wouldn't feel like a great, big sacrifice.*

It proved just how committed he was to being a good father for Sam but it still hurt her.

'You stop acting as though it's torture to take and spend the money I've been putting into your account.'

'I do spend it. Some of it.'

'You buy things for Sam and food for the house. Occasionally you might treat yourself to something cheap and cheerful. I find that insulting.'

'How?' Abigail gasped. 'How can it be insulting if I don't use your money?'

'Take what is given in the right spirit, in the spirit in which it has been given,' Leandro told her bluntly. 'I see you stubbornly refusing what I can give you

and it makes me think that it's your way of telling me
that your pride is greater than your desire to adapt.
I have a certain lifestyle and it makes sense for you
to adapt to it.'

'I suppose you have a point.'

'I know I do. Furthermore, we set a time limit to
this exercise in self-discovery.'

'What do you mean?'

'Here's what I mean.' Leandro didn't beat about
the bush. 'I proposed to you because it was the pre-
ferred solution. Our son would benefit from having
us both there, at hand, rather than being bounced
around between us. You turned me down, and I appreciate that the end result was for you to establish
whether we could be a functioning proposition, but
there has to be a time limit to this probationary period after which we sit down and decide whether we
tie the knot and make this permanent, or else walk
away, knowing that we gave it our best shot.'

Never had she seen more clearly how little love
featured in his life plan that was all set to include
her. Effectively he was telling her that theirs was an
arrangement with benefits, and if, at the end of the
day, the arrangement wasn't working, they'd wash
their hands of it and move on.

'How do you set a time limit on something like
that?' she asked jerkily and Leandro shrugged.

'Good question. It's impossible because there can never been any guarantee that we have reached a point of knowing, for sure, that we are compatible on a long-term basis, which is why I propose we give it three months, at the end of which we decide.'

'Good idea,' she agreed painfully. 'Three months and then, if things haven't worked out, we can go our separate ways and get on with our lives.' She paused and digested this, knowing that it was the best solution and would stop her from drifting hopelessly on uncertain waters, becoming more and more incapable of taking a stand, hanging on to see whether he would one day tell her that he loved her.

Moving out to the cottage felt like a final cutting of ties with life in London. The frantic noise and constant buzz that had been the backdrop of her life for so long gave way to the sounds of nature. Their possessions had been taken the day before by a professional removal company, including furniture from both the apartment and Greyling.

'Cherry pick whatever you want.' Leandro had shrugged. 'And bear in mind that everything will probably be replaced at some point because I can't imagine you'll want to furnish the place in things you haven't personally chosen.'

Abigail could have told him that being fussy was

not a trait she was acquainted with. But she didn't make a song and dance about being parsimonious and being the sort of girl who didn't need to throw money around. She had taken on board what he had said to her and had realised that her continual refusal to accept his lavish generosity was indeed something he found both bewildering and vaguely offensive.

For the first time, she shopped for herself and really enjoyed it.

On her way to the four-wheel drive in which she and Sam but not Leandro would be travelling to the cottage, she paused to look at herself in the mirror.

She'd found her own style. She wasn't interested in flashy designer labels and, left to her own devices, with Leandro's explicit instructions ringing in her ears, she had gravitated towards the clothes she had more or less always worn but this time well cut, well tailored and just that bit smarter. Today, she was in a pair of perfectly fitting designer jeans with designer rips at the knees and a polo shirt with a very small, very discreet logo over the breast pocket. Blue jeans and a white top, accompanied by a pair of flat, tan-and-white leather pumps. She looked *stylish*.

From behind, she registered Leandro strolling towards her, Sam in his arms.

She knew that, to any outsider, they looked as if they could have stepped straight out of the pages of a magazine. She turned and smiled. 'I'm surprised he's not demanding to get down.' Abigail reached out for her son who lunged for her and then, predictably, squirmed until they settled him on the ground. These days he crawled and cruised everywhere with the sort of reckless enthusiasm that kept them both on their toes, sweeping aside breakables and covering sharp corners.

It never failed to amaze her just how naturally those simple things came to Leandro. He had embraced fatherhood. No one could accuse him of not putting his all into it. And by night he embraced the physical closeness that always left her wanting more of him. He was the very essence of what any woman would consider herself lucky to have ended up with. He was as amusing, intelligent and wildly, crazily sexy as he always had been, but scratch the surface and she knew that she wouldn't find the love she desperately wanted.

Never, not once, not even in the heat of passion, had he uttered any unguarded words that could have led her to think that he had the sort of feelings for her that she had for him.

'Want' was a staple in his vocabulary but 'love and need' were ostensibly missing and, with each passing day, she wondered what would happen to them when their three months were up.

He never discussed it and neither did she. She was plagued by the suspicion that she was on trial, and cautious about how she responded, because she knew that what he wanted was a functioning business arrangement and not the sort of complicated emotional involvement that love brought with it.

Deep down she knew that if, at the end of the three-month period, he repeated that offer of marriage then she would accept. They got along, they were bonded in their love for Sam and the sex was mind-blowing. Many marriages worked quite happily on less.

Was she selling herself short? She didn't think so because, whilst she had never envisaged being married to a guy who wasn't madly in love with her, she also couldn't imagine anyone else completing her the way he did.

She wondered whether he would get bored of her and feel tempted to stray but uneasily that was a bridge she was prepared to cross when she came to it.

'Penny for them.' Leandro scooped up his son, leant to brush a kiss on the side of her neck and then held Sam up high until he squealed with laughter, before handing him over to Abigail.

'Just thinking about the move,' she said brightly.

'Sorry I won't be able to come with you now,' Leandro told her. 'but I'll be there later.' He grinned.

'You'll probably get a lot more done without me around,' he told her. 'I would probably get under your feet. Or perhaps just under you.'

Abigail blushed bright red, reminded of just how much he thought about sex, practically to the exclusion of everything else aside from Sam and his work.

Determined not to dwell on what was missing in her life, but to focus on what she had, Abigail spent the drive to the cottage making lots of mental lists of what she would do and how she would apportion her time.

She had been out several times to see it, had supervised the arrangement of the various bits of furniture which had arrived over a period of three days, yet an hour later, when the four-wheel drive drew up in front of the cottage, she was charmed all over again.

The cottage had been upgraded to a very high standard, having been repainted, with new units put into the kitchen and landscaping done in the back garden, as well as hand-made, built-in furniture having been installed in the bedrooms. She and Sam explored the place. She had given the nanny a few days off so that she could accustom herself to the cottage, just Sam, Leandro and her, and as Leandro's driver disappeared back to London Abigail felt the stirring of excitement at this new step in her life.

She allowed Sam to run around the sitting room, where there were no hard edges or glass, then she played with him in the garden and, by the time his afternoon nap time came at one-thirty, he was exhausted.

The kettle was boiling for a cup of tea when the doorbell went and her heart leapt at the prospect of Leandro being here much earlier than anticipated.

She dashed to the door, pulled it open and then fell back in surprise to see Cecilia standing on her doorstep, as stunningly gorgeous as she had been the last time they had seen one another. Both Leandro and his sister shared the same colouring, both olive-skinned with black hair and perfectly chiselled features. Where Leandro's beauty was hard-edged and aggressively masculine, his sister's was aristocratic and intensely feminine. She was the puma to Leandro's tiger. Abigail associated pumas with cunning and danger, which was why she remained blocking the doorway.

'Aren't you going to invite me in?' Cecilia peered past her and took a step forward. 'Great place. I nabbed a peek at the particulars in Leandro's apartment when I arrived a couple of hours ago but it's even better in the flesh. I can see that you've really landed on your feet, Abigail. Must be nice for you, all things considered.'

'Why are you here?' Leandro hadn't mentioned, not even in passing, that his sister was due back in the country today. Had that been a deliberate oversight on his part? Or had Cecilia descended on him without warning?

'To catch up. Why else? I *have* driven all the way from London. The *least* you could do is invite me in for a glass of something.'

'I thought you were in Fiji.'

'Two weeks off. Thought I'd come and see my darling brother. In fact, I just left him with a few things to think about.'

Abigail stilled and she stood aside and quietly invited Cecilia in, guiding her immediately to the kitchen, while the other woman made a big show of looking around her and exclaiming with delight at everything she saw, from the pictures on the walls to the bottle-green range in the kitchen.

'Hats off to you. You've done well. Bet you never thought you'd end up in a fancy cottage with a wad of cash to spend on yourself! Clever of you to get pregnant,' she mused, glancing at her exquisitely manicured nails and buffing them with her thumb before fixing huge, almond-shaped eyes on her.

Abigail didn't say anything, instead turning away and taking her time to make a pot of tea. Her heart was hammering and she knew, with a sickening feeling, that this conversation was going somewhere and the destination wasn't going to be very nice.

But, now that the other woman was in the cottage, she had little option but to travel down the circuitous route of icy small talk laced with sugar-coated insults. She bit her tongue. There was no way that she was going to open up a can of worms by getting into an argument with Leandro's sister.

'He tells me that marriage is on the table,' Cecilia said abruptly. They were sitting at opposite ends of the cleverly weathered wooden table, which had had pride of place in the kitchen at Greyling, and Abigail nodded and met the other woman's eyes squarely.

'We feel that Sam would benefit from having both of us around.'

'Stop talking about yourself and my brother as though you're a *couple*,' Cecilia hissed. 'You're *not* a couple. You weren't then and you aren't now.' Her eyes welled up. 'I knew you were trouble the minute you met Leandro the first time round. He barely had time to talk to me when you appeared on the scene!'

Concerned, Abigail flew to her feet and rummaged in her handbag which she had slung on the kitchen counter, extracting a wad of tissues and shoving them over to Cecilia.

'I should have known that something was up when he sent me halfway across the world to oversee that hotel in Fiji.' Her voice wobbled but the glare was intact. 'It was impossible to talk to him, what with the time difference and the problems with the Internet! But I found out everything today when I confronted him. You are *not* going to marry my brother. You are *not* going to take him away from me.'

'I—I'm not planning on taking him away from you,' Abigail stammered.

'He doesn't want to marry you!' Cecilia's voice had risen and Abigail worriedly glanced at the kitchen door, which was open. The last thing she needed was a shouting Cecilia and a screaming toddler. 'You're all wrong for Leandro and the last thing he wants is to *marry* you.'

'Did he tell you that?'

'Of course he did!' Cecilia shouted. 'We discuss *everything*! He told me that you're forcing him to marry you because of the kid. He told me that you're not really his type. He doesn't *care* about you. He doesn't *love* you!'

Abigail looked down. Cecilia had a vested interest in saying all those things, in causing as much chaos as she could. But was she lying? She was only confirming what Abigail already knew.

She expected another shrieking tirade from the other woman, and was rising to her feet to forestall that by leading her firmly out of the cottage, when

Leandro's voice from the doorway of the kitchen stopped her in her tracks.

She hadn't heard him enter the house. Of course, why would she? He had a key and she had been entirely focused on Cecilia. She wouldn't have noticed two yetis if they had walked past the kitchen door holding hands.

'Cecilia.' Leandro's deep voice was cool, as was the gaze arrowing towards his sister as she spun round, reddening before rushing to his side. But before she could hug him he held out his arms to stop her. 'What are you doing here?'

'I—I came to say hi to my nephew,' she stammered, 'but *she* wouldn't let me.'

Abigail opened her mouth to protest and then was overcome by a feeling of deep hopelessness. Why would Leandro believe her? He didn't love her. It was going to be just as it had been nearly two years ago when he had listened to Cecilia and refused to give Abigail a fair hearing. He had been judge, jury and executioner to their relationship and why would it be any different now?

Perhaps he had already been persuaded that without love he was better off without her, whatever he said about wanting to stay with her because of Sam. Perhaps he might have drifted into a relationship with her, but he was no doubt open to being persuaded by Cecilia. Abigail could easily envisage a situation where she managed to convince him that there was someone better for him out there, someone who shared the same background, someone he could love rather than like, and with whom the ties would not be centred around obligation and duties to an infant he had never asked for.

Her imagination was running riot but through all that she couldn't help but notice that he wasn't chastising his sister. Indeed, he was drawing her to one side, although his eyes were firmly focused on Abigail.

'I'll make sure Cecilia gets back to London,' he said without any inflection in his voice at all that could have given her a clue as to what he was thinking.

Which made her fear that he was already thinking the worst of her. He had descended out of the blue to be told that she was the cruel woman withholding a nephew from his aunt. Cecilia could work a sob story like an Oscar-winning actress.

And yet, in receipt of a sly look from the other woman as she was gently led out of the kitchen, Abigail couldn't help a pang of sympathy for her. That plaintive voice had been real. Cecilia was hurt because she had felt ignored by the big brother who had always had time for her. The hint of tears had not been phoney.

Not that any of that changed anything. The three months might barely have started, but if Leandro could not give her the benefit of the doubt now, and remain behind to hear from her exactly what had transpired between herself and his sister, then he would never be prepared to give her the benefit of the doubt over anything.

In short, nothing had fundamentally changed between them since he had turned his back on her all that time ago, except that he was now a father. His attitude towards her remained the same.

He would hand-deliver Cecilia back to London, all those protective instincts that had been fostered since youth would kick into gear and he would indulge his sister and whatever lies she chose to tell him.

Lord knew, he would probably head straight back up to the cottage to fling another one of his *terms and conditions* in her face, specifically one banning her from upsetting his sister.

Suddenly weary beyond belief, Abigail went out into the garden and headed straight for the lovely gazebo that had been erected under one of the fruit trees. Sam's window was flung open and she knew that she would be able to hear him should he wake up and start crying, although his afternoon naps were long, and she knew that he wouldn't be up for at least another hour.

Precious time during which she would try and get her thoughts in order, try and reach a conclusion to the ebb and flow of life as she had recently been living it.

Her thoughts became muddled as she closed her eyes. It was a fine day, the breeze just the right side of warm. Nature had its own sounds and with her eyes closed she could really appreciate all of them. The sound of the leaves in the trees rustling, the birds chirping and, in the distance, the roll of traffic because although the cottage was in the middle of nowhere this was something of an illusion, because the road to London was not terribly far away.

Drifting into a light doze, she had a dream of Leandro walking away from her and, with every panicked step she took closer to him, the faster he moved away, glancing back towards her and walking on even though he could see that she was upset.

She started violently when his deep, familiar voice said, way too close and way too vibrant to belong to a dream, 'Falling asleep in the sun is never a good idea.'

Abigail's eyes flew open and she gaped. 'I thought you were dropping your sister back down to London!'

'She came in a car,' Leandro said drily, 'and there's no reason why she can't return in it—although my driver brought me here, so I've had him deliver her back down and leave my car here.' He stood where he was, hands in his pockets, his dark, beautiful face revealing precious little.

He looked away briefly, and when he raked his fingers through his hair she finally identified that unrevealing expression on his face for what it was. Discomfort. Since she had never seen him out of his depth, that was a piercing cause for concern, and suddenly all the doubts and insecurities she had nurtured under the surface rose to the top, clamouring to be heard.

Heart in her mouth, she cleared her throat and said quietly, 'I think we should have a chat. I'm not sure what your sister told you, Leandro, but she did tell me what you said to her about… Well, put it this way, about your heart not being in making this relationship work, and it's no big deal.'

'It's not?'

'It's nothing that I didn't know, and I want you to know that I really appreciate the effort you've made in trying to stay together for Sam's sake. It was never going to happen, of course,' she said ruefully, lowering her eyes. 'You can't fit a square peg into a round hole, which is what we have been trying to do. I'm sure you'll agree with me.'

She looked at him and flushed because he was

staring at her with such a curious look of hesitancy that she didn't know whether to carry on in the same vein, shift course or bolt for the back door.

She did none of those things. Instead, she plastered a smile on her face and prompted, 'Well? Say something, Leandro. Because Sam is going to be up soon and if we have to have this talk then this is the best time to have it…'

CHAPTER TEN

'I HAD NO idea that Cecilia was going to show up at my apartment today. At least, not without warning.'

'But you spoke to her on the phone.' Abigail restively stood up and began heading into the cottage, because outside was for relaxing and she wasn't feeling relaxed. She was aware of Leandro following her. It made the hairs on the back of her neck stand on end. 'She must have told you,' she carried on, swinging round to look at him, hand on one hip. 'I mean, she made it clear that you tell each other *everything*.' This last was slung at him in an accusatory voice and Leandro glanced away, jaw tensing.

When had all his control started seeping away? Control was the one thing he had always aimed for. Control in his professional life and control in his private life. When had that all disappeared? Could he have stopped it somewhere along the way or was it just a process that had begun when Abigail had first entered his life, a process that had simply been temporarily halted when she had left, only to continue the moment she'd returned?

He certainly didn't feel in control now. He felt… like any red-blooded man would feel if he had one foot dangling off the edge of a precipice.

She sat down at the table but was staring off into the distance.

'She has always been dependent on me,' Leandro explained heavily. 'Our parents had little time for us and Cecilia relied heavily on me for pretty much everything. Of course, as time went on, I assumed she was becoming more independent, and certainly on the surface she had a good life. She never wanted for anything and she had a lot of friends. She still came to me for advice. She still confided in me. I found it amusing, and I suppose it was a comfort zone that worked. She did her degree, immediately started working for my organisation in the hospitality field and she was, and is, excellent at it.'

He sighed and linked his fingers together. 'I never really noticed how possessive she was of my relationships, because I took everything at face value, and they were never meaningful. When you came along…'

'When I came along,' Abigail filled in for his benefit, 'she couldn't wait to blow it out of the water because she wasn't in control of it.'

Leandro's mouth quirked. 'She couldn't wait to blow it out of the water because she sensed that it could become serious,' he corrected quietly. 'She sensed something I myself wasn't even really aware of. I wanted you the minute I laid eyes on you, Abigail.'

'So you told me,' she responded with an edge of bitterness in her voice. 'I've always known that. You want me and you find me attractive. You'd be surprised how insulting that can feel after a while. It was heady when we first met. I'd never met anyone like you in my entire life. How would I? You moved in the sort of circles I would never have been allowed to enter. I've said this before but I'll say it again— that was why I kept quiet about my background. I wanted to enjoy you without all those judgements being formed about me because of where I'd come from. Cecilia must have thought that she'd struck gold when she dug and found out all that stuff about me.'

'I should have listened to my conscience,' Leandro admitted, 'instead of accepting the evidence against you and jumping to the wrong conclusions.'

'What are you saying?' Abigail looked at him defiantly because she refused to get her hopes up. She'd had them dashed too many times.

'I was wrapped up with you, Abigail. I don't know how it happened, because I always thought I was well protected against emotional involvement, but you managed to work a way through to me… Maybe that was why I was so quick to pigeonhole you as a gold-digger. You'd lied, and it was easy and lazy to believe the worst of you, because if I didn't I would have had to admit to having feelings for you that went way beyond wanting to have sex with you.'

Abigail's heart leapt. 'I didn't tell you I was pregnant because I knew what you thought of me…'

'I understand. When I saw you again, I realised that I still wanted you,' he confessed. 'I'd just broken up with someone who, on paper, should have been the perfect match. Cecilia introduced us.' He grimaced. 'I suppose at that point I should have read the writing on the wall and realised how important it was to my sister that she should never feel threatened by any woman I chose to date.'

Abigail allowed herself a glimmer of a smile, because if there was one type of reading Leandro didn't do it was reading writing on the wall. She could understand that because, if you never dug deep, you never found yourself out of your depth.

He stood up and paced the kitchen, vaguely taking in the small steps she had already made towards turning it into a home. There were two framed pictures of Sam on the wall by the table and some herbs in pots on the window ledge. She'd done the same when she'd been living with him. She had somehow transformed his apartment in incremental ways, from a cold space to something homely, and she'd done it without him even really noticing.

'I heard what she said to you,' he stated flatly. 'It was impossible not to overhear because she wasn't making the slightest effort to keep the noise levels down.'

Abigail tensed and stared at her linked fingers on the kitchen table.

'I had no conversation with her along the lines she intimated. I should be furious that she should take it upon herself to come here and purport to be my mouthpiece, but I'm not.'

'Because she paved the way for you to…tell me what's been obvious all along?'

'Something like that.' He reached out and held her fluttering fingers still until she was forced to look at him. 'This is hard for me to say,' he told her in a low, driven voice. 'I've never believed in love. I have always associated it with something destructive. I thought I was immune to its effects but I was wrong.'

'What do you mean?'

'I mean I was half way to falling in love with you the first time round, and this time round I've managed to complete the job. I'm head over heels in love with you, Abigail, and I think I've known that deep down for some time now.'

'You're in love with me?' she whispered, eyes as round as saucers.

'I buried it under the excuse of rising to the occasion and doing the right thing, but when I proposed I should have asked myself how it was that I wasn't appalled at the change it would bring to my cherished lifestyle. I was blind and I drove you away.'

'You drove me away because I wanted so much more than you were offering. I wanted the whole package. I wanted you to love me the way I loved you.'

She smiled at him and he returned her smile, relief mingled with satisfaction.

'I never allowed myself to feel confident around you,' she confessed. 'I was too aware that we came from opposite sides of the tracks. I was scared when you got that call from Cecilia,' she carried on, 'because I could project and see the damage she had done being done again. When you left with her again earlier on today, I was convinced that the next time I saw you it would be to learn that you'd decided to take the road away from me, the road I'd paved for you to take. I had a lot of principles about marrying for the right reasons. I mean, I wanted my future to be completely different to my past. I wanted the whole package deal—romance and love with all the trimmings. Except I fell in love with you and there weren't any trimmings. I felt I couldn't walk into a union with someone for the wrong reasons and, somewhere along the line, I decided that perhaps you would start to feel the same things I felt.'

'Will you marry me, my darling?'

Abigail nodded, stood up and moved to sit on Leandro's lap. She curved her hands around his neck and drew him to her. 'Of course I will. Believe it or not,' she conceded sheepishly, 'I was desperate for you to pop the question again because marrying you—even if you couldn't love me—felt a whole lot better than the alternative, which was not having you in my life.' After a pause, she said, 'What about your sister?'

'She won't be back to air her views,' Leandro said shortly. 'I will, naturally, continue to see her when she happens to be in the country—but she overstepped the boundaries and that's unacceptable.' He sighed deeply. 'Protecting my sister has become a habit over the years and it's blinded me to some of her failings. She will continue to run my hotel in Fiji but she won't be bothering you in the future. Now, let's stop talking about Cecilia and let's start talking about…*us*.'

EPILOGUE

ABIGAIL GAZED AT her reflection in the mirror with a smile of satisfaction because this was exactly how she had wanted to look. Not flashy, no overkill, but not so understated that she could have been going to a cocktail party.

This was the perfect wedding dress. It was straight and simple, with exquisite silvery beading against the cream background. The neckline was modestly scooped while the back dipped a little lower. It was the last time she would be able to fit into something as tight as this—she was ten weeks pregnant and she could already spot the incipient signs of an expanding tummy.

Tonight, she would tell Leandro, and she couldn't wait to see his face when she broke the news. He had missed out on her being pregnant with Sam and she knew that he would be the most attentive husband, lover and father-to-be with the baby she had found out she was carrying only a few days ago.

That would be surprise number one.

Surprise number two would be his sister. Cecilia had been firmly put in her place and given her marching orders, to hold the fort on the other side of the world and never again to interfere in his life. Abigail knew Leandro and, whilst he was the fairest man she could ever have hoped to meet, he was not a guy who believed in beating about the bush.

When he had informed her that he had told his sister to cease and desist, Abigail had very quickly imagined a terse and unapologetic two-sentence conversation. Whatever Cecilia had done, it was fair to say that she had done so against a backdrop of issues that had made her overly dependent and fragile and therefore vulnerable to the thought of her brother no longer having time for her.

A week ago, Abigail had spoken to her on the phone. The conversation had been awkward, halting and, at least to start with, defensive on the part of Cecilia, but Abigail had persevered and two days previously, unbeknown to Leandro, Cecilia had arrived in London. They had met and Abigail had taken Sam along with her.

'You're his aunt,' she had said gently, 'and it's important that you get to know him. Every child needs a fun aunt. I've seen the movies.'

Cecilia had offered a grudging smile, but after five minutes she was no longer holding Sam with outstretched arms as though he were a parcel that might contain hazardous bio-waste material.

Abigail wouldn't go so far as to say that they had bonded at first sight, but Rome wasn't built in a day.

And, just at the moment, everything was looking pretty wonderful. Leandro had no idea that his sister would be attending the wedding. Abigail drily thought that, for a man who notoriously hated surprises, he was in for a fun-filled day and evening.

From behind, she saw Vanessa enter the room with a smile and low wolf whistle.

She grinned. 'I think that the groom is going to be a very happy man when he sees his radiant bride.'

Abigail turned around, mirroring her friend's smile with one of her own,

'Let's go,' she said, smoothing down the fabulous dress and allowing Vanessa to put some finishing touches to the beads in her hair. The stylists and the beauticians had gone and this was going to be her last few moments as a single girl. She knew that there was no one she would rather walk down the aisle to than Leandro. 'The rest of my life is waiting.'

* * * * *

If you enjoyed
THE SECRET SANCHEZ HEIR,
why not explore these other
Cathy Williams titles?

WEARING THE DE ANGELIS RING
THE SURPRISE DE ANGELIS BABY
SEDUCED INTO HER BOSS'S SERVICE
SNOWBOUND WITH HIS INNOCENT
TEMPTATION
BOUGHT TO WEAR THE BILLIONAIRE'S RING

Available now!

#3541 THE SECRET KEPT FROM THE GREEK
Secret Heirs of Billionaires
by Susan Stephens
Damon Gavros and Lizzie Montgomery's searing desire sweeps her back to their exquisite night eleven years ago! But Lizzie's hiding something, and Damon's determination to discover it is relentless. Until he finds out Lizzie's secret is his daughter!

#3542 THE BILLIONAIRE'S SECRET PRINCESS
Scandalous Royal Brides
by Caitlin Crews
Princess Valentina swaps places with her identical twin, but she quickly realizes that fooling her "boss" Achilles Casilieris is going to be difficult when he makes her burn with longing. Their powerful attraction will push Valentina's façade to the limit...

#3543 WEDDING NIGHT WITH HER ENEMY
Wedlocked!
by Melanie Milburne
Allegra Kallas both *detests* and longs for Draco Papandreou, so she's horrified when he's the only man who can save her family's business. Draco has a sinful plan: he'll make Allegra his wife and seduce her into his bed...

#3544 CLAIMING HIS CONVENIENT FIANCÉE
by Natalie Anderson
When Catriona breaks into her old family mansion to retrieve an heirloom, she doesn't expect to get caught by Alejandro Martinez! Kitty's recklessness ignites Alejandro's animal urges. So when Kitty is mistaken for his fiancée, he'll take full advantage—and unleash their hunger!

---

*Ariston Kavakos makes impoverished Keeley Turner a
proposition: a month's employment on his island, at his
command. Soon her resistance to their sizzling chemistry
weakens! But when there's a consequence, Ariston makes
one thing clear: Keeley will become his bride...*

Read on for a sneak preview of
Sharon Kendrick's book
THE PREGNANT KAVAKOS BRIDE

ONE NIGHT WITH CONSEQUENCES
Conveniently wedded, passionately bedded!

"You're offering to buy my baby? Are you out of your
mind?"

"I'm giving you the opportunity to make a fresh start."

"Without my baby?"

"A baby will tie you down. I can give this child everything
it needs," Ariston said, deliberately allowing his gaze to drift
around the dingy little room. "You cannot."

"Oh, but that's where you're wrong, Ariston," Keeley
said, her hands clenching. "You might have all the houses
and yachts and servants in the world, but you have a great
big hole where your heart should be—and therefore you're
incapable of giving this child the thing it needs more than
anything else!"

"Which is?"

"Love!"

Ariston felt his body stiffen. He loved his brother
and once he'd loved his mother, but he was aware of his
limitations. No, he didn't do the big showy emotion he

suspected she was talking about, and why should he, when he knew the brutal heartache it could cause? Yet something told him that trying to defend his own position was pointless. She would fight for this child, he realized. She would fight with all the strength she possessed, and that was going to complicate things. Did she imagine he was going to accept what she'd just told him and play no part in it? Politely dole out payments and have sporadic weekend meetings with his own flesh and blood? Or worse, no meetings at all? He met the green blaze of her eyes.

"So you won't give this baby up and neither will I," he said softly. "Which means that the only solution is for me to marry you."

He saw the shock and horror on her face.

"But I don't want to marry you! It wouldn't work, Ariston—on so many levels. You must realize that. Me, as the wife of an autocratic control freak who doesn't even like me? I don't think so."

"It wasn't a question," he said silkily. "It was a statement. It's not a case of if you will marry me, Keeley—just when."

"You're mad," she breathed.

He shook his head. "Just determined to get what is rightfully mine. So why not consider what I've said, and sleep on it and I'll return tomorrow at noon for your answer—when you've calmed down. But I'm warning you now, Keeley—that if you are willful enough to try to refuse me, or if you make some foolish attempt to run away and escape—" he paused and looked straight into her eyes "—I will find you and drag you through every court in the land to get what is rightfully mine."

Don't miss
THE PREGNANT KAVAKOS BRIDE
available July 2017 wherever
Harlequin Presents® books and ebooks are sold.

www.Harlequin.com

HPEXP0617

HARLEQUIN
Presents®

Next month, look out for the final installment of the thrilling
The Secret Billionaires trilogy! Three extraordinary men
accept the challenge of leaving their billionaire lifestyles
behind. But in *Salazar's One-Night Heir* by
Jennifer Hayward, Alejandro must also seek
revenge for a decades-old injustice…

Tycoon Alejandro Salazar will take any opportunity to expose the
Hargrove family's crime against his—including accepting a challenge
to pose as their stable groom! His goal in sight, Alejandro cannot
allow himself to be distracted by the gorgeous Hargrove heiress…

Her family must pay, yet Alejandro can't resist innocent Cecily's fiery
passion. And when their one night of bliss results in an unexpected
pregnancy Alejandro will legitimize his heir and restore his family's
honor…by binding Cecily to him with a diamond ring!

The Secret Billionaires

Challenged to go undercover—but tempted to blow it all!

Di Marcello's Secret Son
by Rachael Thomas

Xenakis's Convenient Bride
by Dani Collins
Available now!

Salazar's One-Night Heir
by Jennifer Hayward
Available July 2017!

Stay Connected:

www.Harlequin.com

[f] /HarlequinBooks

[t] @HarlequinBooks

[p] /HarlequinBooks

HP06080

Get 2 Free Books,
Plus 2 Free Gifts—

just for trying the Reader Service!